The Everyman Wodehouse

P. G. WODEHOUSE

# Kid Brady Stories

and

# A Man of Means

(with C. H. Bovill)

EVERYMAN

Published by Everyman's Library
Northburgh House
10 Northburgh Street
London EC1V 0AT

*Kid Brady Stories* first published in *Pearson's Magazine*, New York,
September 1905–March 1907
*A Man of Means* first published in *The Strand Magazine*, London,
April–September 1914
Published by Everyman's Library, 2013

Typography by Peter B. Willberg

ISBN 978-1-84159-189-6

A CIP catalogue record for this book is available from the British Library

Distributed by Random House (UK) Ltd.,
20 Vauxhall Bridge Road, London SW1V 2SA

Typeset by AccComputing, Wincanton, Somerset
Printed and bound in Germany
by GGP Media GmbH, Pössneck

# Kid Brady Stories

# CONTENTS

## 1 KID BRADY, LIGHT-WEIGHT

It had begun to snow. The policeman who was looking after Chinatown muttered an Irish oath which lost itself in his huge blonde mustache, and quickened his pace, wishing that he were off duty. Chinamen flitted to and fro in their furtive way, or stood gesticulating in groups at the corners. It was growing dusk.

The boy turned out of Pell Street in the aimless way common to those who are conscious of having many hours before them and no obvious means of passing them. He was a trim-built little fellow, but thinner than he should have been. That was because his meals were irregular, and not large even when he got them. A man in a shop had given him half a loaf that morning, which was a stroke of luck; but that had long since gone the way of all loaves. He was feeling hungry again now. That was why he lounged into Mott Street and stationed himself before the shop of Yen Lo. Somehow he never felt so hungry when he looked at the food in the window. Chinamen have quaint tastes in the matter of feeding. Yen Lo's window was full of the gruesome carcasses of pigs. There were also certain fishes, pickled. Years had passed since they swam into the net. The smell of them was like the smell of the lion-house in Central Park, but more emphatic. The boy felt as he looked at them that there might be worse things than hunger.

A kick roused him from his reflections, not the powerful kick of an enemy, but the affectionate kick of a friend, the equivalent of a tap on the shoulder. He looked around to find the tall policeman towering over him.

'Well, sonny, what's doin'?'

'Nothin' doin'.'

'Go to that man I told you wanted an office boy?'

'Yep.'

'Wasn't he wantin' any of you?'

The boy shook his head mournfully. The tall policeman had been very good to him. Ever since they had struck up their queer friendship a month before, he had been fertile in suggestions for the boy's advancement. Every time they met he had some new proposal which was to put him on the high road to fortune and a brownstone house on Fifth Avenue. Somebody was wanting an office boy, or perhaps a boy to run errands; a hotel needed a new bell-boy. There was no end to his well-meant suggestions. But nothing ever came of them. The places were always filled by the time the boy applied for them, and he was beginning to feel that he should never find one. He lived – somehow – from day to day. It had been difficult at first, when the death of his parents had flung him on his own resources, to wring a living out of the iron city. But he had managed it. The charity of the poor to one another is as wonderful in New York as in other big cities.

His history was of a common kind; he was English by birth, but his father, who had suffered from the popular superstition that America is a country where dollar bills grow on trees, had sold the small Devon farm to emigrate to the United States. He had found, like a great many others, that the United States did not particularly want him. And now he was dead, and his wife too; and the boy was alone.

The policeman strolled off, and the boy, having temporarily quelled his hunger by means of the scent of the pickled fish, moved on into the Bowery.

As he turned the corner he blundered into a man who was walking swiftly along the street, muffled in a huge overcoat.

'Now then, ye young devil,' said a deep voice not unkindly.

The man recovered his balance and was about to walk on, when he caught sight of the boy more distinctly and paused in astonishment. His costume was certainly not in keeping with the season. Winter and summer he wore nothing but a red shirt and a pair of very old breeches, though he sometimes, as at the present moment, added a still older pair of shoes to his equipment.

'Ye're cold?' boomed the man from the depths of his greatcoat.

The boy supposed, on reflection, that he was; but he had not noticed it particularly until now. He was used to his costume. But now that it was brought home to him by a direct question, he realized that his vague feeling of discomfort was due to that cause.

'Yep,' he said.

'Why don't ye go home?'

'Haven't got a home,' replied the boy shortly.

The man regarded him with a compassionate stare.

'Here,' he said.

He unbuttoned his coat, produced a coin from his pocket, and passed on at a swinging walk.

The boy examined the coin. It was a half-dollar. He stood looking at it, almost dazed. He had never handled specie in the bulk before.

As he stood there his eye was caught by something small and black on the ground. It was a pocket-book; and as he picked it up he saw that it was stuffed with greenbacks. As long as there had been anybody to do it, the boy had been well brought up, and remnants of what he had been taught remained with him. He had a rigid code of honesty, and not for a moment did it occur to him to appropriate this treasure that had apparently fallen from the skies for his own special benefit. He must find the big man in the overcoat and return the pocket-book. As a preliminary step, he would consult his friend the policeman. Meanwhile, being passing rich with half-a-dollar in his pocket, he would fill himself as full as one might for fifteen cents, and put by the remainder for the morrow.

Officer O'Gorman took charge of the pocket-book next morning, and commended the boy's sagacity in entrusting it to an able and intelligent officer.

'Oi'll take ut to the station,' he said, 'and when we've found who it belongs to, ye climb in sharp, sonny, and get the reward. Why—'

He broke off with an exclamation of surprise. 'Mike Mulroon!' he said. 'Bedad, now if that's not remarkable! Ye're in luck, sonny. I was just goin' to tell ye to scuttle to Mike Mulroon's to ask for the "Boy Wanted" which he's put on his door, an' here ye're introducin' yerself to him without my knowin' it. See, here's his name in the pocket-book. Ye run round to his gymnasium, sonny, an' give him the long green an' tell him you're the boy he's been advertisin' for. Ye know Mike's gymnasium ?'

The boy nodded. Mike Mulroon, toughest of middle-weight boxers in his day, which was now past, had set up a gymnasium on retiring from active work, and now devoted his time to teaching the noble art and training fighters for their battles. Every boy in the Bowery knew Mike by reputation, and secretly longed to follow in his footsteps. It was an unexampled piece of good luck that he should be able to present himself with such an excellent argument in his favor as the returned pocket-book, just when Mike was wanting a boy for his gymnasium. He started to run, but, recollecting that he was a monied man, stopped after he had reached the Bowery, and sprang on a car, where he had the perfect joy of putting the conductor to utter rout by presenting him with his fare. The conductor was a man who had little faith in human nature as represented by the youth of the Bowery, and he judged people by their exteriors. He thought the boy was stealing a ride, and said so.

'You had better be careful, me man,' said the boy haughtily, as he paid over the five cents.

Mulroon's gymnasium was in Sixteenth Street. The boy charged in like a thunderbolt, to find the stalwart Michael engaged in sparring with a gilded youth who looked as if he had been in the habit of sitting up late.

The round came to an end, and Mike looked around.

'Well,' he said, 'an' what can I do for you?'

'Please, Mr Mulroon,' said the boy rapidly, in the manner of one speaking a piece, 'you dropped this last night when you gave me half-a-dollar and I picked it up, and Mr O'Gorman says it's got your name in it so it must be yours, so I've brought it and there ain't any missing. And Mr O'Gorman says you want a boy here, and will I do?'

'Bai Jove!' said the gilded youth, who had once spent a summer in London, and wished people to know it, 'Bai Jove, smart boy that, really smart!' Mike Mulroon took the pocket-book in silence. The exhibition of honesty in one who was young enough to know worse had quite overpowered him.

'I'm much obliged to you,' he said at length.

'And can I be the boy wanted?'

'What can you do?'

'Anything.'

'Well, you can't want more than that, Mulroon, eh?' said the gilded one, 'and he's honest, bai Jove. Here, kid, help me out of these bally pudding-cases, and I'll give you a dollar.'

Thus did the boy enter upon his duties at Mike Mulroon's gymnasium.

At first these were not extensive, nor was his pay; but both were greatly to his taste. He speedily fell into the ways of the gymnasium, and after a few weeks Mike began to feel that he could not get on without him. By the combination of an agile brain and a strict attention to business the boy made himself indispensable, and between Mike and himself there sprang up a friendship which was destined to last. Mike had all the Irishman's fondness for children, and as for the boy he worshiped the ex-champion as only a boy can worship a man whose muscle has won him fame. There were scores of boys in the Bowery who would have boasted of it for weeks if the ex-champion of the middleweight had spoken a couple of words to them. To be with him all day on the footing of an honored assistant was almost too much happiness.

In this way he passed the next four years of his life, drinking with his every breath the exhilarating atmosphere of the ring. It was small wonder that his ambitions were limited to the only profession of which he knew the ins and outs. He understood vaguely that there were in the world soldiers, and politicians, and artists, and that other boys had their eyes set on these professions as a goal; but for himself, his tastes lay in another direction. He wanted to be a fighting-man. There had been a feverish time, after a visit to Weber and Field's theater, in the days before that famous partnership was dissolved, when he had wished to go on the stage. But learning from Mike that it was quite the fashionable thing for a first-class pugilist to take to the boards, his ambitions had veered around again to the ring, where they remained.

It was when he was sixteen, two years after his introduction to the gymnasium on Sixteenth Street, that his prospects of realizing his ambition began to grow brighter. Until then, greatly as he desired to do so, he had not been able to bring himself to ask Mike to take him in hand and educate his fists. He had to content himself with watching the tuition of others, and imitating the blows as best he could from memory.

But one day he arrived at the gymnasium in a state that commanded the attention even of the usually unobservant Mulroon. One of his eyes was closed, and his face wore a generally damaged expression.

'You've been fightin', kid,' said Mike, proud of his penetration.

'Yes,' said the boy. During his two years at the gymnasium he had observed the speech of the gentlemen who came there, and had pruned his own of the little growth of dialect which had grown on him.

'Did ye win?'

'No.'

There was a pause.

'I can't fight,' said the boy despairingly; 'I don't know how. Couldn't you teach me, Mike?'

'Tache ye!' said Mike. 'If ye've got it in yer, I'll make a champeen of ye. But I'll wait till ye've got two eyes to see by.'

And the boy retired, hugely delighted, to put raw steak on his injuries.

From this time his progress may be said to have been fairly steady and continuous. He was a pupil of the sort that Mike loved best, quick and active, willing to learn, and with no shadow of fear of punishment. From being 'Boy Wanted,' he was promoted to the post of assistant instructor. When more than ordinarily enervated youths came to the gymnasium to be built up, preparatory to plunging once more into a whirl of cotillons and late suppers, they were turned over to the Kid, as more suited to their powers than the massive Mike. And occasionally when some fighter came to train with Mike for a battle, the Kid was allowed to act as one of the sparring-partners. So he acquired speed and knowledge, and learned by experience the difference that lies between the amateur and the professional.

It was two days after his eighteenth birthday that, arriving a little late at the gymnasium, he found Mike in conversation with a tall, wiry-looking young negro.

'Here, Kid,' said Mike, as he sighted him, 'come here. Ye've read of Mr Van Courtlandt's unknown which is to fight Eddie Brock next month? This is the lad – only it's a secret, so ye mustn't tell – Joe Johnson, colored champeen of Brooklyn at the light-weight limit. Ye'll be one of his sparrin'-partners.'

The Kid shook hands with the stranger. Being British-born, he had none of the American's inherited dislike of the colored, but there was something in the Brooklyn man's face which he did not fancy. His early life in the street had given him the habit of summing up the men he met at a glance.

Training work began that day, and with it a feud between the Kid and the colored man. In his first bout the former after being severely handled – for the Brooklyn champion was evidently not one of those boxers who play light in a training-bout – succeeded in planting a jab with his left on the mark, always a weak spot with negro fighters, which put an abrupt end to the encounter.

Johnson, as he rose to his feet again, shot a venomous glance at his antagonist. From that day onward every bout between the two was a pitched battle. Mike, unobservant as ever, did not notice any particular malice on the part of his man, but merely saw what he took to be a promising vigor. At the end of each day's training the Kid ached as if he had been through a stiff fight in the roped ring. Incidentally he, too, began to train. It was evident to him that only fine condition could enable him to hold his own. Thus it came about that two men were getting into shape under Mike's care.

And as events turned out, this was fortunate. This match between Eddie Brock and an unknown was one that was exciting considerable interest in sporting circles. Brock was a rising light-weight, and was supposed to have claims to the championship. This fight would decide his merit. Nothing remains secret for very long in New York, and it was generally understood, though unofficially, that the colored boxer, Johnson, was to be his opponent. Johnson was known to be a clever, resolute fighter, and it was thought that if Brock could obtain the decision over him, his backers would be justified in trying to arrange a match for him with Jimmy Garvis the Californian, the light-weight champion of America. A good deal of money would be won and lost over the present contest.

About a week before the fight, the Kid, walking home after his day's work, met Officer O'Gorman. Four years had had no effect on their friendship.

'An' how is yer unknown?' inquired O'Gorman, after they had exchanged greetings.

'Oh, fine,' said the Kid. 'Well inside the weight, and strong. He loosened a tooth for me today. Mike tells me not to give it away that Johnson's the man who's to fight Brock; but, there, what's the use? Everybody knows.'

Officer O'Gorman tapped him mysteriously on the chest and lowered his voice.

'An' I'll tell ye somethin' which everybody doesn't know,' he growled through his mustache.

The Kid looked interrogative.

'An' that is that 'ere Joe Johnson won't win,' said the policeman.

'Well, I've not seen Eddie fight,' said the Kid, 'but he'll have to be a warm proposition to put it over Johnson.'

'He'll not win,' proceeded O'Gorman, 'bekase he manes not to win.'

'What?'

The policeman nodded.

'Sure. We cops get next to the game easier than most. We hear things. There's bin framing-propositions made to him. He's bin paid to lose, an' it's up to him to do ut. He's buncoed ye, Kid.'

'How do you know?' cried the Kid. 'How did you hear?'

Officer O'Gorman displayed a coy reticence.

'Mustn't tell pro-fessional secrets,' he said. 'But you may stand on me. On the wor-rud of a mimber of the city police. So don't ye go puttin' yere long green on the wrong man, Kid,' he concluded, paternally.

The Kid was a man of action. He was early at the gymnasium next day. The colored representative of Brooklyn was alone in the room, punching the bag with bare fists in a meditative manner. He did not look up when the door opened.

The Kid came straight to the point. He was not fulsomely polite.

'You black beast!' he said, 'so you've been playing double.'

The colored man's reply was swift and direct. He wheeled around on the Kid, and his thick lips parted in a grin of rage.

The next moment he sprang in like a flash with both arms working like flails.

The Kid side-stepped to avoid the furious rush, and put in a left hook which brought his man up sharp. The black rushed again, landing heavily on the Kid's ear. It was the last blow he delivered. As he came in to follow up his advantage, the Kid spied an opening. His right shot across, and Mike Mulroon, opening the door at that moment, was just in time to see the colored champion collapse in a heap like an empty sack.

'What the – Kid, is ut crazy ye are?'

The Kid wrenched himself free.

'Let me go, Mike,' he cried angrily.

'But what in the worruld do ye mane by knockin' our man about just before his fight?'

'Yes, bai Jove,' said another voice, which the Kid remembered, 'it certainly requires explanation. I'm Mr Van Courtlandt, my lad. What do you mean by man-handling my nominee like this?'

The Kid faced him.

'You've been buncoed, sir,' he said excitedly. 'Johnson never meant to win. He's been got at. I was telling him that I knew, and he rushed at me.'

'And how do you know?'

For the first time the Kid realized that his evidence was, to say the least, thin.

But he had not to produce it. As he stood wondering how to begin, the prostrate negro suddenly rose and rushed through the door, banging it behind him. He had come to during the conversation and had remained where he lay, waiting for events to develop themselves. Apparently in his opinion they were not developing themselves satisfactorily, and he thought it best to quit a scene which promised neither profit nor pleasure.

Mr Van Courtlandt stared after him blankly.

'There, sir!' said the Kid in triumph, 'don't that show it?'

'It does,' admitted Mr Van Courtlandt pensively, 'it does. But,' he added, 'it does not show me how I am to find a boy who really will beat Master Eddie.'

'Try the Kid, son, try the Kid. Ye needn't fear he'll not do his best. An' he's as good a lad with his hands as ye'll need to see.'

'Well,' said Mr Van Courtlandt, 'he was certainly good enough for the lamented Master Johnson. Then may I rely on your services?'

'Proud, sir,' said the Kid.

'An' I'll bet,' put in Mike, 'six to four with any man in four-spot wafers that my Kid gets the decoration.'

And as was subsequently proved in fifteen rounds and part of a sixteenth, he could not have made a sounder investment.

Hear what Mr Robert Fitzsimmons says, heavy-weight champion of the world until the star of Jim Jeffries rose and eclipsed him: 'If I were preparing a man for an important fight,' he states, 'I would allow him to read the daily papers after breakfast for an hour.' Mike Mulroon held the same view. In the first week of his training he gave the Kid the Sunday edition of the *Manhattan Daily* to read. And the Kid read it. And that was how all the trouble began.

The Kid slipped his left glove neatly over Peter Salt's guard and into that gentleman's earnest, serious face. Peter Salt, who had the twofold reputation of being a persevering middle-weight and the most silent man connected with the Ring, had come to White Plains to take some of the burden of the Kid's training off Mike's shoulders.

He took the blow without emotion, and swung around his right for the Kid's ribs. But the Kid, as quick on his feet as a kitten, had side-stepped out of danger before the blow arrived. Once more his left shot past Peter's guard, as he ducked out of the corner of the gymnasium, into which the determined rushes and extra weight of the silent one had forced him. Out in the middle of the floor Peter was helpless. The Kid was in and out and in again with that wonderful straight left of his, and the other's heavy returns wasted themselves on air. 'Time,' said Mike Mulroon from his place by the window. 'Kid, ye're in rare shape today.'

'That upper-cut of Peter's is goin' to put me out of business one of these times,' said the light-weight modestly.

Peter said nothing. He was engaged in delivering scientific hooks at the punching-bag, by way of rest and relaxation between the rounds.

A year had passed and a great many stirring things had happened since the Kid had made his first appearance in the roped ring. He was now a person of importance. His victory over such a noted man of his hands as Eddie Brock had given him a reputation, which he had maintained and increased. Mike had proceeded with caution in his arrangements with regard to the Kid's professional career. There were many, after his fight with Brock, who considered that the new man should have been matched at once with Jimmy Garvis, the champion. Mike, however, preferred to feel his way. A championship fight is a big thing for a novice to undertake. The Kid had certainly shown splendid form against Eddie Brock, but it needs more than one trial to prove a man a world-beater.

He took advantage of the fact that Jimmy Garvis was on a tour through the States with a theatrical company, to arrange a match with Wallis, the Denver light-weight.

The great Jimmy had beaten Wallis in eight rounds. It took the Kid seven.

When the champion returned from his tour, flushed with the applause of the multitude and bursting with pleasantly-earned dollars, he found that his title was urgently required of him by a young gentleman of New York, whose very name he did not remember ever to have heard. Jimmy's manager, a business-like young man, who chewed gum, talked the thing over with Mike, while the champion, in a fur-lined coat, sat on two chairs and smoked a cigar a size smaller than his walking-stick.

If this Brady person of whom Mike spoke meant business, said the manager, and if the purse was of that bulk which we like to see in purses, and if he was not required to scale less than a hundred and forty pounds at the ring-side, his man would be only too charmed to accommodate him. He referred to his principal.

'Does it go, Jimmy?' he asked.

'S-u-u-ure,' drawled the great man amiably, reaching out with his foot for a third chair. And the thing was settled.

From the very beginning of his training, the Kid had done all that man could to meet Mike half-way. He was desperately in earnest about this fight. He realized that it meant everything to him. Once let him win the championship, and he was a made man. If he lost it again a year later, he would at least have been at the top of the tree for a while. Even an ex-champion commands respect.

But he did not mean to lose if he could once win it. His heart was in his profession. Like most pugilists he was something of a philosopher. He was of opinion that it was a better thing to seek fortune in a twenty-foot ring than to work for wages in a shop. The moral aspect of the trade did not trouble him. He felt no more enmity toward Jimmy Garvis than Jimmy felt toward him. He took it for granted that the other man objected to hard blows as little as he did himself.

He threw himself into his work with a single mind. Peter Salt had instructions to hit as hard as he liked – or could – and the Kid took the stiffest punches with an imperturbable cheerfulness which promised well for his coolness in the hour of battle. In a word, everything was running as smoothly as possible until that copy of the *Manhattan Daily* fell into his hands.

It was at nine fifteen, precisely, on Sunday morning that he read the article which was the cause of his undoing. He had risen at eight as usual, and had gone through a dumb-bell exercise with one pound bells, a couple of rounds with Peter Salt, a salt-water sponging, and an energetic rubbing-down. After that he had made a simple but pleasant breakfast of oatmeal, eggs and a chop. He was now basking in the sun on the low veranda of the Wheatsheaf Hotel with his Sunday paper in his hand, wondering lazily what Jimmy Garvis was doing with himself at this hour by the sad sea waves at Atlantic City.

After a while he dismissed Jimmy from his thoughts, and turned his attention to the paper.

He chuckled over the colored comicalities of the humorous supplement, skipped an indignant article about a gas bill, gazed with interest at a misty photograph of himself on the sporting page, and finally began to read a column of the magazine section headed 'Is Steak a Mistake?' to which was appended as a subtitle 'Eat more Fruit, say Doctors.'

He read idly at first, but soon his face grew serious and his attention became riveted. It was a specious little bit of writing, the work, evidently, of a clever man. The author, building up his case with considerable skill, and marshaling his points with excellent judgment, set out to show that the habit of eating meat was ruinous to the constitution. He instanced the Japanese, who attained to great strength on a diet of rice. He peppered his article with the names of various vegetarian athletes. Most of his arguments were old, but the Kid had never heard them before, and they electrified him. Instead of getting into condition, he felt he had been lowering his constitution and throwing away his chances of success by eating meat every day. And twice a day! It was not an hour since he had taken a great chop. The recollection chilled him. He read on.

It seemed that the writer, while deprecating meat, was not satisfied with mere vegetarianism. He went further. He advocated a diet consisting exclusively of fruit. He urged that what was natural must be the best. Cooking, he said, was unnatural, and therefore wrong. 'Man's natural diet was fruit, and nothing but fruit. It is the opinion of the medical men who lead the new thought that the man who feeds exclusively on fruit is healthier, happier, stronger, and has far greater powers of endurance than the ordinary man.'

'Powers of endurance,' murmured the Kid to himself, thinking of Jimmy Garvis's famous rushes. He would need all the powers of endurance at his disposal to stave them off. Could fruit be the secret of victory?

'It purifies the blood,' continued the writer, 'and clears the eyes. The old idea of building up strength on beefsteak is out of date. Fruit is a thousand times better. I cannot close this article more suitably than by transcribing the recipe for health given by Mr Alexander Pontey, the famous fruitarian. "Begin," he says, "gradually. Eat a pound of Brazil nuts, some almonds and raisins, and six or seven bananas for breakfast; more bananas, half a dozen apples, and a fruit pudding midday; with a milk pudding and as many apples, pears, and raisins at night as you can eat. You can drop the puddings as you get on." In those words are contained the secret of Perfect Health.'

The paper fluttered to the ground.

'Gee!' whispered the Kid, astounded.

It was at the moment that Mike Mulroon came out into the veranda.

'Mike,' said the Kid, 'you're not trainin' me right.'

Mike looked shocked and horrified.

'What!' he shouted.

'You're giving me meat, and I've no use for meat. It isn't right. I ought to be taking fruit.'

Mike stared.

'Fruit?' he repeated in a dazed manner. The Kid put the paper into his hand, and indicated the important article. Mike sat down and began to plow slowly through it. He was not a rapid reader; on the other hand, he did not skip, and when he returned the paper to the Kid he had read every word of the column.

'Well?' said the Kid. 'So you see.'

Mike was perplexed. He said nothing.

'You see,' continued the Kid earnestly, 'I've been wasting strength all the time instead of putting it on. And I'm getting slower instead of quicker.'

This roused Mike to protest.

'You're quick enough,' he said. 'Whatever y'are, ye're quick.'

'I should be quicker still,' retorted the Kid, ignoring the compliment, 'if I'd the right feed. But it's only the first week, an' there's plenty of time to change it. Here's what I'll have. Pound of Brazil nuts. And almonds and raisins. And some bananas. That'll be breakfast. I'll cut out this bit, an' keep it, so we shan't forget what I'm to have.'

Mike's bewildered eye, roaming to and fro, lit on Peter Salt seated in the room behind the veranda with a paper.

'Peter,' he called.

Peter looked up, and came out to him.

'Peter,' he said, 'here's the Kid says he wants to give up mate of all description, and train on fruit.'

Peter looked thoughtfully at the Kid, and shook his head.

'Shouldn't,' he said.

'You don't understand,' cried the Kid, 'and Mike, he don't understand. It's what doctors say. Here's this man Pontey – Alexander Pontey. The famous fruit – fruitarian they call him. That means he's no farmer. He knows his business. He's a dead sporty mug, and listen what he says.'

And once more he read out the recipe for health. 'You see. That's a man who knows. He's to the good. He's no farmer. What he says goes. Don't eat meat, he says, but fruit, and you'll beat the world.'

Peter Salt lit a cigar and grunted. To those who knew him well all his grunts had their special meanings. This one, being translated signified 'My dear, good young friend, you may be a clever fighter, but here you are talking straight through the center of your hat.'

Mike interpreted it correctly, and, encouraged by support, endeavored to overcome the Kid by argument.

'This Pontey,' he said—

'Alexander Pontey,' added the Kid, dwelling on the name reverently.

'What's he done?' demanded Mike.

'He's a famous fruitarian,' said the Kid, warily, on his defense.

'Yes, but what's he done, Kid? Here's me. I've trained bhoy after bhoy for fights on good mate, an' I've fought meself – eighteen battles – on mate. An' all my bhoys, bar wan or two, have got the decision, an' I won thirteen of me battles. And on what, mind ye? On mate. An' what's your fruit gazebo done? Is he a champeen? Nit! Has he trained champeens? Not wan. Show me one bhoy that's won a fight on fruit, and I'll show ye twilve that's done it on mate. Now, Kid, what do ye say to that?'

He slapped his leg triumphantly as he delivered this *coup de grâce*. But the Kid, who had slipped many a knock-out punch in the ring, did so now in argument.

'Ah,' he said, 'but you're forgetting, Mike, that the others, the ones your men beat, were trained on meat, too.'

For five minutes, while Peter Salt sat unmoved in his seat, blowing smoke rings, and gazing absently across the square at the gymnasium opposite, Mike wrangled with the Kid. But he was fighting a losing fight. He could not recover from that counter with which his opponent had replied to his best argument. At the end of five minutes he sat back, and mopped his forehead. 'Well,' he said despairingly, 'if you must, you must.'

For, being an experienced trainer, he knew that a man getting into condition for a fight must be led, not driven. And after all, there was just a chance that the unorthodox method on which the Kid had set his heart might do him good. One of the best trainers who ever trod New York pavements has put it on record that there are no rules for training a man. Individuals and their physical needs vary as widely as do the seasons. What sets one man up would break another down. Apples and bananas, which would have reduced Mike himself to a wreck in a week, might turn the Kid into a world-beater.

But it was with a marked lack of enthusiasm that he went out that afternoon to make his purchases. The energetic citizen from whom he bought the Brazil nuts was left with the impression that he had either suffered some sad bereavement, or that he had begun to feel gloomy respecting the chances of his man in the fight with Jimmy Garvis. After much thought he favored the latter reason, and proceeded to back the Californian heavily. And Mike, with the bag of nuts in his hand, went back to the hotel to prepare the Kid's lunch.

For the first two days the new system answered, to all appearances, admirably. The Kid was such a whole-hearted convert to fruitarianism that the diet worked on the faith-cure system. He hypnotized himself into believing that he was gaining strength and quickness, and on the evening of the second day, put in a left-right on Peter Salt's jaw with such emphasis that the latter himself became a temporary and unwilling fruitarian, and dined off oranges and apples, chopped small. But on the third day came the reaction. He lost weight, not healthily and by slow degrees, as a man in training should, but with a rush.

'At this rate,' said Peter Salt, startled by the figures into a whirl of eloquence, 'there won't be enough of you left on the day to go into the ring.'

And Mike, lifting up his voice, cursed the man who invented Brazil nuts.

The Kid was sitting on the veranda on the afternoon of the fourth day, brooding over his loss of form, and wondering whether perhaps Mike's old-fashioned, out-of-date diet was not, after all, as good as any other, when there entered to him, from the road, a young man in a light flannel suit. On the back of the young man's head was a Panama, and in addition to these articles of clothing he wore that indescribable air of jaunty self-confidence which is the peculiar property of the New York newspaper young man. It is a curiously compelling air. The most reticent man becomes confidential beneath its influence. Trust magnates, fascinated by it, babble forth their most shady secrets.

'Mr Brady, I believe,' said the young man.

'Sure,' said the Kid.

The young man drew up a chair, sat down, and tilted his hat over his eyes.

'We've met before,' he said, 'though you don't remember me. But don't apologize. We can't all be celebrities. I interviewed you after your fight with Eddie Brock. Garth's my name. Tom Garth. I'm on the *Manhattan Daily*.'

'Sure,' said the Kid. 'I remember you now. Have a cigar?'

'If you guess again,' said Mr Garth. 'You'll be wrong. Well,' he continued, throwing away the match, 'you've been doing great things since our last merry meeting. I've got two dollars on it that you'll stop Jimmy in a dozen rounds. Remember that, when you get into the ring, and let it inspire you. How are you getting on here?'

'Bully,' said the Kid.

'No difficulty in getting down to the weight?'

'Dead easy.'

Mike Mulroon came out on the veranda, and was introduced.

'Looks pretty fit,' said Garth, jerking his head at the Kid.

Mike grunted disconsolately.

'Now, I've come here,' said Garth, 'professionally. Our sporting editor wants a story about you for tomorrow, Mr Brady. It will appear in company with alleged comic pictures of you by our artist, but these are things which must be borne patiently. We all have our troubles. I should be glad if you would answer a few questions. Peter Salt is sparring with you, isn't he?'

'Yes.'

'He's a good man. Saw him smother Martin Morse in a couple of rounds once in San Francisco.'

The conversation turned on Peter's ring exploits.

'Now about yourself,' said Mr Garth. 'Once more into the breach, dear friends, once more. What do you feed on? That's what the public wants to know. What do you eat?'

'Fruit,' said the Kid.

'Fruit!' snapped Mike.

'Yes?'

Mike stared stonily before him.

'What else?' asked Garth.

'Nothing,' said the Kid, 'only fruit.'

'What!' said Garth. 'Nothing?'

The Kid shook his head. The interviewer's eyes opened.

'Well,' he said at length. 'I don't want to set my opinion up against yours, and you probably know best what's good for you, still – fruit. Well, it'll be the first time a man has won a championship on that, I'll bet.'

Mike glanced at him with awakening hope. Here was a newspaper man, and so likely to be handy in an argument, backing up his own opinion on the great fruit topic.

'The Kid,' he said, 'will have it that fruit is what a bhoy should train on, an' he's killing himself with it.'

'So I should think. Whoever heard of training on fruit!'

The Kid produced his trump card, and prepared to play it.

'You're wrong. It purifies the blood, an' makes you strong. Dr Pontey says so.'

Mr Garth sat up.

'Dr which?' he said.

'Dr Alexander Pontey. It's all wrote here. Read it.'

Tom Garth took the newspaper cutting, and burst into a roar of laughter. The Kid eyed him with grave disapproval.

'Do you mean to tell me that you've been converted to fruitarianism by that article? You dropped meat simply on the strength of that?'

'Sure,' said the puzzled Kid.

Tom Garth rose to his feet.

'Now, look here,' he said, 'before I say a word I must ask you to promise not to hit me. I enjoy life, and have no wish to be hustled out of it prematurely. Will you promise not to let your angry passions arise?'

The Kid looked at Mike, and Mike looked at the Kid. They were not feeling equal to the intellectual pressure of the conversation.

'What—' began the Kid.

'Promise,' said Garth, 'go on, promise!'

'I promise,' said Mike.

'Me, too,' said the Kid. 'It's not up to me to start in jolting people.'

'Then,' said Garth, 'listen. I wrote that article, and it's meant to be funny.'

'What!'

'But so subtle and delicate is my humor that apparently the thing is misleading. Our magazine editor wanted something light last Sunday, so I did that. And you thought it was serious! Why there isn't a word of sense in the thing. You'll remember you promised not to hit me, won't you.'

The Kid clutched at his last straw.

'But Dr Pontey—'

'There isn't such a man. I got him out of a book. I tell you the whole thing's absurd from start to finish. Read it again, and you must see. And you've been living on fruit on the strength of it. Oh, Lord! It's lucky I turned up in time, or you'd have gone into the ring a wreck – if you hadn't died before. But why on earth didn't you ask a doctor, if you thought of changing your diet?'

Mike had been standing open-mouthed during this speech, and now he essayed a comment. But the thought of those wasted days in which the Kid had been going back instead of forward in his training, proved too much for him; his jaws snapped like a trap, and he strode off without a word.

At seven that evening the ranks of the fruitarians lost a proselyte.

## 3 HOW KID BRADY WON THE CHAMPIONSHIP

Clancy's Saloon in the Bowery is not far from the one made famous by Bishop Potter, but it differs largely in character from its neighbor. It is looked on with suspicion by the police, who consider it, in the vernacular, a 'pool-joint.' In other words, a great deal of gambling goes on there. Indeed, the attentions of the Force are so marked that Clancy, who is something of a humorist, has often thought of exhibiting in his window the notice, 'Please wipe your boots before raiding.' There is nothing much known against Clancy himself. The quarrel the police have with him has to do chiefly with the company he keeps, for his patrons include some of the most finished scoundrels in New York.

Some days before the date fixed for the Kid's fight with Jimmy Garvis for the championship, three of the saloon's older customers sat at a little table near the bar. Like everybody else in the city they were discussing the coming battle.

'Say, Kid's gone up in de betting,' said one of the three.

'How?'

'Sure. Six to four.'

The two speakers were typical products of the Bowery at its worst. There is nothing innately vicious about the Bowery atmosphere, hundreds work and live honestly in that noisy quarter; but it is apt to produce citizens who are of no extreme value to the community.

The third of the trio was higher in the social scale. He had a certain air of refinement. He looked as if he was accustomed to move in a somewhat loftier sphere of life. He was, as a matter of fact, something of a celebrity in his own line. Until recently he had been making a good income by card-sharping on Atlantic liners. His face was familiar in the smoke-room of many a *strasse* hotel. It was to prevent its becoming too familiar that he was now taking a brief holiday on shore. His occupation was thus to a great extent gone, for it is only on liners that that child-like trust which the poker player so admires in his fellow-man is to be found. Players in New York were keener, and the resultant gains smaller. The best holiday being a change of occupation, he had temporarily abandoned cards, and was now endeavoring to make both ends meet by means of the Higher Finance. He had betted heavily against Kid Brady, and he meant to insure himself against loss.

'So much the better for us,' he said. 'I wish I could find some rub who'd give me a hundred to four. The bigger the odds are, the more we win. We can't lose.' The man who had spoken first looked cautiously around, and was reassured to find that nobody was within earshot.

'Say,' he whispered, 'what's doing? I ain't next to de game.'

'It is perfectly simple. Brady is not going to fight.'

'On your way! What's to keep him?'

'I thought I had made that clear. If you must be told again, listen now. I happen to know that the Kid will be in Carson City at least two days before the fight. He is to stop at Pauley's. Mike Mulroon will be with him, and Peter Salt. They have engaged rooms. We must go, too, take rooms at the same hotel, kidnap him, and keep him till after the fight.'

'But, say—'

'Yes, yes,' said the other impatiently, 'you're going to say that it can't be done. It can be done. It will be difficult, but it only requires care. I know the number of the Kid's room. It is seventy-three, on the second floor. Mulroon and Salt are sleeping in seventy-four, across the passage. I have been there and talked to the hotel clerk. Two other rooms in the same passage are vacant. I telegraphed for them today. Now, listen. On the night before the fight the Kid will go to bed early. Mulroon and Salt will see him to bed, and then go down-town or to the smoking-room. That will be our time. We let him get to sleep, go to his room—'

''Twill be locked, sure.'

'That won't keep us long. We get in, chloroform him, and carry him down the passage to one of our rooms. There we tie him up and keep him, and one of you will stay in the room and guard him. Lock the door, and don't let anyone come in. I will tell them that you're ill, and not to be disturbed.'

'But if de Kid doesn't fight,' objected one of his companions, 'all de bets'll be off.'

'I shall look after that. You can make your minds easy about the bets.'

'Put us wise, mister.'

'Not yet. You shall know when we get to Pauley's. Not till then. I'm taking no risks.'

It was Peter Salt who had insisted that the Kid should stay at Pauley's on the night before the fight. There was a grain of superstition in Peter, and his belief in the luck of Pauley's amounted to a craze. Certainly past events justified it. The house had never sent a loser into the ring. Jack O'Neil had stopped there on the night before he beat Smith, the Australian middle-weight. Frank Willard had used it as his headquarters on three separate occasions and each time he had won. It had not been a difficult matter to persuade Mike Mulroon that a couple of nights at Pauley's spelt victory.

So thither the Kid went with his guardians, and from the day he arrived the hotel began to do double business. The bar-room was crowded every night with sportsmen who hoped to see the Kid and judge of his form before placing their money. But Mike, whom habit had made wary in these matters, kept his man close, started on the daily walk from the back of the house, and did the necessary sparring in a private room behind locked doors. His spare time he spent in receiving interviewers from all cities – for all the leading journals had their men on the spot – and inform-ing them that the Kid had never felt better in his life, but was seeing no visitors. So the newspaper men had to go away content with that, and wire highly imaginative and worked up articles to their editors on *What Mulroon Thinks*.

Jimmy Garvis, in the meantime, housed at the Hotel Splen-did, two blocks down the street, made no secret of his inten-tion of putting it all over his opponent, as he phrased it. Public opinion wavered. But the betting continued six to four on Brady until the morning of the last day of waiting. Nobody appeared to know what had changed it. No new reports had come in as to the men's form. But at mid-day even money was being offered and taken, and in the evening Mulroon, repairing to the bar after seeing his man to bed, found people, who certainly looked perfectly sane and sober, offering ten to six against the Kid. And other people, equally sensible to all appearances, were fighting shy of taking the odds.

Mike had the courage of his convictions. He had seen Jimmy

Garvis fight, and he had seen the Kid fight, and he had never been so convinced of anything in his life as of the superiority of the latter. For skill there was no comparison. The champion was a willing fighter and had no objection to taking whatever his man liked to give him, provided he could put in something of his own in exchange. He was all pluck and muscle. But the Kid was there with the goods when it came to science. Unless one of the champion's fierce swings came home on a vital spot, his man must win.

His Irish blood was up. He joined the gathering at the bar, and took every offer that was made. His confidence led others to follow his example, and gradually the odds were reduced. By that time the finances of Mike were in a perilous position. His liabilities, if the Kid were to lose, would sweep away the savings of a busy life. For a moment he thought of hedging. Then he set his jaw and turned away. It was an insult to himself to think a man he had trained and watched over could be beaten so contemptibly. He believed in the Kid, and he would back his belief to his last dollar. But he was mopping his forehead as he left the bar at midnight to take a last look at his man. He turned the handle of Room 73 softly, and peeped in.

'Sleepin' like a baby,' he murmured, and went off to bed, content.

It was not until the following evening that he began to have apprehensions. During the day the Kid had remained in bed, dozing. He was well below the weight agreed upon in the articles of the battle, so that it would not matter if he was to put on a couple of pounds before he entered the ring. In fact, Mike generally liked his men to begin their fight a shade on the heavy side. He had seen too many fail through being over finely drawn.

But when the time approached for the contest, for the first time he could not restrain a doubt. Somehow the Kid did not look that picture of all that was fit and well which he had presented to a small, but select and admiring audience on the previous evening. There did not seem so much of him.

He was, moreover, taciturn. He did not speak a word from the time he rose from his bed. To Mike's occasional questions he replied with grunts. Peter Salt himself could not have been less conversational. This, however, did not trouble Mike to any great extent. The Kid had always relapsed into a more or less unbroken silence on the day of a fight, and Mike had respected the eccentricity of genius and refrained from bothering him with talk.

But the matter of his weight was more serious. Instead of having put on a couple of pounds, he had lost five. And when a boxer suddenly loses weight at the end of a course of training, it is ominous.

Looking at him, too, Mike could not resist a feeling that there was something missing, something more than a few pounds. A man in perfect training seems to diffuse an atmosphere of electricity from within. There is an indefinable something about him which tells the practiced eye that he is exactly fit, that physically nothing more can be done to improve him. Yesterday the Kid had worn this air. Today he had lost it. He did not look unhealthy, but he certainly did not look as if he had been training for a month.

These things Mike's mind perceived dimly, but sufficiently clearly to make him feel gloomy and ill at ease.

'Hwhat is ut?' he said to Peter Salt, as he had said on another occasion when the waywardness of the Kid's mood had caused him discomfort. 'Do ye see anything, Peter? Is the lad well?'

Peter Salt shrugged his shoulders. He, too, had noticed the alteration.

'He looks,' he said slowly, 'as if he'd been doped.'

Mike started. The thing was incredible. Yet cases had been known where a pugilist had been drugged on the eve of a contest.

'Peter, it can't be! My heavy hand on the man that did it.'

'Doctor,' said Peter briefly. Mike saw his point. A doctor would examine the men before they entered the ring. If drugs had been administered, he could not fail to detect them.

Half an hour later his fears were dispelled. The doctor passed the Kid without hesitation. He looked very keenly at him, however, and after the examination he did a thing which would have disturbed Mike Mulroon not a little if he had seen it. He sought out a sporting friend, and unostentatiously betted twenty dollars with him, giving the odds, that Jimmy Garvis would retain the championship. 'If a man in that condition can put it over Jimmy, I'll eat my stethoscope,' he said to himself. 'What on earth can Mulroon have been doing to him? Why, the boy's not trained worth a cent!'

The hall was filling rapidly now. All sorts and conditions of men were shuffling their way past the knees of those already seated, and establishing themselves in their places; men in evening dress, looking prosperous and comfortably excited; men in blue jerseys, smoking villainous cigars and shouting greetings to distant friends in strange dialects. Here and there an impassive black face showed up among the white. At one side of the ring was the reporters' table. Keen-faced, weary-eyed young men sat here, nibbling pencils and drawing idly in note-books. The atmosphere was charged with smoke.

A man in evening dress clambered with an effort into the ring, to be greeted with a round of applause and cries for silence.

'Gentlemen,' he shouted, 'I must ask you kindly to stop smoking.'

The effect of this request on the audience was not remarkable.

A few conscience-stricken sportsmen threw down their cigars hastily and ground the lighted ends under foot, but the majority continued to smoke, though for the most part in a furtive manner behind a protecting hand. The referee, having got his request off his mind, did not seem to care about pressing the point. He made a signal to someone invisible in the passage that led to the dressing-rooms, and the next moment a roar of welcome sent the smoke-cloud swirling, as the champion, clad in a long blue bath-robe, ducked under the ropes, and seated himself with a bow and a grin in the farther corner. And the roar greeted the Kid, in a pink bath-robe. Each pugilist was attended by three companions, burly and jersey-clad. Mike Mulroon and Peter Salt, in the Kid's corner, came in for a special cheer on their own account.

The referee climbed into the ring again. Dead silence reigned in all parts of the building. 'Gentlemen, this is a fight between Jimmy Garvis of California' – a wave of the hand toward the farther corner, a shout of applause from the audience, and a gratified bow from Mr Garvis – 'and Kid Brady of New York' – another wave of the hand, and renewed cheering – 'for the lightweight championship of the United States. The fight is for—' He paused. 'I must wait,' he said in a pained voice, 'until those gentlemen at the door are quiet.'

For what seemed to be a bye-battle on a small scale had suddenly begun at the entrance to the hall. Two doorkeepers were struggling with a third man, and a group had gathered around to watch.

'Silence! Order! Bounce him!' roared the justly indignant hall.

From the center of the struggling group a voice made itself heard.

'Mike!' it cried. 'Mike! Mike Mulroon!'

Mulroon literally sprang into the air. He stood gasping.

'Go and tell your friend, Mr Mulroon,' said the referee severely, 'to be quiet, or he must leave the hall. He is interrupting the proceedings.'

There was a crash. One of the doorkeepers flew back against the wood panel. A small, compact figure darted past him and flung himself into the ring.

'Friend!' shouted Mike Mulroon. 'But, friend! By the Powers, 'tis the Kid himself!'

The noise was deafening. Everybody in the building was standing, everybody was shouting. The man in the pink bath-robe made a dive under the ropes, but Mike was too quick for him. He seized him in a grip of steel. Two policemen, stationed at the ringside, closed in on the captive, and hustled him out of the hall. The referee stood in the middle of the ring, sawing the air with his hands in a fruitless appeal for silence. Beside him stood the Kid, panting and disheveled, but himself beyond the shadow of a doubt. The howls died away.

'Gentlemen,' said the referee rapidly, 'in the whole course of my ring experience I have never met a case like this. Some one has been playing it on us. There has been foul play. If you want to know who the man I introduced to you just now really is, you had better read your newspaper for the next few days, when he will be up in court. I can tell you who he is not. He is not Kid Brady. This is Kid Brady.'

Applause.

'Gentlemen, under the circumstances I must crave your kind indulgence. The championship fight will be postponed for half an hour, to enable Brady to put on his fighting clothes. During the intermission Tom Allen will spar with Joe Watson. Gentlemen, I thank you most sincerely.'

The Kid's story did not take long to tell. He had wakened, he said, with a bad taste in his mouth, to find himself in a strange room, with a gag between his teeth and ropes around his hands and ankles. After several hours' labor he had loosened these, and taking advantage of the fact that his warder, wearying probably of his charge, and thinking that he could trust the ropes to guard the prisoner, had left the room, he had freed himself, broken the lock, and escaped. That was all he knew.

The rest came out at the trial. It seemed that the Kid's double was an out-of-work actor who had consorted with the baser kind of sporting man, and had thus fallen in with the astute card-sharper who patronized Clancy's Saloon in the Bowery. The latter had seen the possibilities that lay in his resemblance to the Kid. With a little make-up, such as the actor knew well how to apply, their best friends could hardly tell them apart. His scheme was simplicity itself. The 'double' would appear in the ring as the Kid, be summarily despatched by the unsuspecting Mr Garvis, and thus win for the confederate the extensive bets he had made. But for the Kid's unexpected reappearance, nothing could have prevented the success of the plan.

As for the fight – if you read the sporting pages in the papers you will know all about that. There were columns describing how Jimmy Garvis, going in to hit from the first sound of the gong, had the best of the opening rounds, nearly put his opponent out in the fifth, and ended the sixth with a distinct balance of points in his favor; how he seemed to weaken in the seventh and eighth; and, finally, how in the second minute of the ninth, the Kid, pulling himself together, sent in a blow with his right which made him light-weight champion of America. For the details, picturesque as only an American journalist can make them, the reader is referred to these official reports.

The Kid's first act after becoming champion was to open a
saloon on East Fourteenth Street. His second was to buy an automobile. There are three stages in the career of the successful
American pugilist. He begins obscurely, fighting hard with the
rank and file of the profession and endeavoring, in the intervals
of active work, to induce friendly newspaper men to put photographs of him in defiant and scientific attitudes into their papers,
together with eulogies on past deeds and glowing prophecies
respecting future matches. Then, having begun to make a name,
he starts a saloon, and, finally – the last test of prosperity – he
buys an automobile (which he refers to as his 'bubble') and begins
thoroughly to enjoy life.

One evening, some months after his fight with Jimmy Garvin
– who was now shrieking challenges at him in the evening papers
in the hope of obtaining a return match – the Kid was in his
saloon, leaning against the counter with the air of careless majesty which is a characteristic of the successful fighter, and watching the austere barmen serve the customers who poured in. He
was proud of his saloon, and with some justice, for it was orderly,
well-appointed, and well patronized. The prize-fighters' saloons
of New York are by no means the noisy, sordid dens which those

who do not know them imagine them to be. They are as clean as pins, and as decorous as A.B.C. shops. Nobody had a word to say against Kid Brady's saloon, if we except Mrs Carrie Nation, who, according to the papers, had bought a new hatchet and announced her intention of paying the Kid a professional visit in the near future.

But the champion light-weight of America was not the man to let a trifle like this worry him, and as he leaned on his counter he felt at peace with mankind, even with Jimmy Garvin. It was, he felt, purely the etiquette of the profession that had led that gentleman to describe him in a letter to a sporting weekly as a 'skunk.' It was a mere conventional pleasantry, and showed no animus on the part of the defeated one.

To him while in this enviable frame of mind there entered a boy.

'A letter for you, Mr Brady,' said the boy, with respect.

The Kid extended a hand for the missive. The messenger meanwhile stood eyeing him with intense reverence. It was not his luck to come frequently to such close quarters with the famous light-weight, and already, by handing him the letter, he had done enough to make himself a marked boy in his set. If he could but lure the great man into a conversation, however brief, his reputation would be made. The Kid examined the note curiously before opening it. His correspondence was not large, and what there was of it was not written, as was this letter, on the gold-stamped paper of the Hotel Universal. Also, it was delicately scented, and the scent was not tobacco.

He opened it, and glanced first at the signature. 'Catherine Beaumont.' A lady! Here were mysteries and marvels.

'Dear Mr Darrell,' it began.

Now, one of the Kid's minor weaknesses was that he liked to

be addressed as 'Mr Darrell.' 'Kid Brady' was merely his professional pseudonym. His real name was Edward Darrell, and socially he liked to be called by it. Persons who endeavored to win his regard by addressing him publicly as 'Kid' would have done far better to have called him 'Mr Darrell.'

The letter itself was a little unusual:

I have heard so much about you from my brother James, whom you taught to box last year, that I feel no diffidence in writing to you. I am in dreadful trouble. I need a *strong* man's help *immediately.* My brother is in San Francisco. I have no friend in New York. Do *please* call *at once* at this hotel. I shall remain indoors for the rest of the evening.

CATHERINE BEAUMONT

PS – The boy will carry an answer.
PPS – It is a matter of the *utmost* importance.

The Kid's comment was brief but emphatic.

'Gee!' he said.

'Any answer to de letter, Mr Brady?' inquired the messenger by way of a conversational opening.

'You go back, sonny, and say how I'm comin' at once. Now see if you can make the hotel in two jumps.'

The boy darted off, storing these golden words in his mind, to be retailed later to an admiring circle of his peers.

As for the Kid, he went upstairs and put on his best clothes. This was a special occasion. The somewhat emphatic tweed suit which he affected as a rule must give way to something more nearly resembling what the Four Hundred wore when they paid calls. He selected a dark serge, hovered a few moments over a batch of neckties, and, deciding finally in favor of a dark green, thrust a smart pin into it, and made his way to the Hotel Universal.

He remembered James Beaumont well – a man of some standing in New York society, who had come to his gymnasium to work off the effect of a strenuous course of dinners at Sherry's and Delmonico's. One of the evening papers had caricatured him in an imaginary contest with the Kid, who was then just beginning to achieve fame.

Miss Beaumont's suite was at the top of the hotel. Deposited by the elevator opposite the door, he knocked and entered a neat sitting-room.

Seated in a chair at the farther end of the room was his correspondent. In his own circle of society the Kid was by way of being something of a ladies' man. A fighter is always popular with the other sex. He was what is called in the vernacular a 'strong josher.' In other words, he always had plenty to say for himself. But here was a lady of another sort. To judge from a first glance, she was the sort of lady whose portrait was in all the papers when she went to the Horse Show. He got a blurred impression of a beautiful face and an exquisite dress, and then he lost his head.

'Mr Darrell? Please sit down.'

The Kid sat down, dimly realizing that he ought to have done something which he had left undone. Later it occurred to him that the lady had offered her hand, and he had not taken it.

'It was so kind of you to come so promptly.'

'Yes, Miss,' said the Kid.

'But I was sure you would. My brother spoke so highly of you.'

'Yes, Miss.'

'I am in great trouble, Mr Darrell.'

'Yes, Miss.'

Here it suddenly struck the Kid that he must pull himself together. He was rattled. His remarks, he felt, lacked variety and brilliance.

'I'm sure,' he said, with an effort, 'I'm sure – anything I can do—'

He lost the thread of his discourse, and came to an abrupt stop. A drop of perspiration splashed on his wrist.

Fortunately the mind of woman is conducted with an eye to these emergencies. Miss Beaumont was tactful. It was plain that the Kid was in a parlous state, and that it would be brutal to look for conversation from him for some time to come. He sat there on the edge of his chair, fingering his hat in an overwrought manner, and gazing earnestly at the carpet. His hostess put him at his ease. For the space of three minutes, she delivered a monologue on a variety of unimportant topics in a sweet rippling voice which acted magically on the Kid's disturbed nerves. At the beginning of the fourth minute he surprised himself by volunteering a statement. It was not very profound nor very original, but it was a statement, and he began to feel confidence slowly returning. Before the fourth minute had elapsed he was himself again.

'I can explain in a very few words, Mr Darrell, just what it is that I want you to do for me, if you will be so kind.'

Five minutes before the Kid's head had swum at the idea of this gorgeous being condescending to be under an obligation to him, but now he positively waved his hand deprecatingly, just as he had seen the star do at Daly's, when the leading lady had insisted that he had a noble soul.

'It is very kind of you, Mr Darrell. I am sure a man in your position must be extremely busy. What I want is this: Tomorrow morning I start from the Central Station to join my brother in San Francisco. I want you to be there to look after me.'

The Kid politely placed his 'bubble' at the lady's disposal. She thanked him, but declined.

'I must not put you to any more trouble than I can possibly help,' she said. 'It will be quite enough if you meet me on the platform at half-past eleven. My train leaves at twenty-five minutes to twelve.'

'I'll be there, miss,' said the Kid.

There was a pause. It was now the lady who gazed at the carpet, and looked embarrassed. The Kid was wondering whether the interview was at an end, and whether he was supposed at this point to make a graceful exit, when Miss Beaumont, blushing in an effective manner, hesitated, and finally spoke.

'I think I must tell you everything, Mr Darrell,' she said. 'It will explain what you are probably thinking is extremely curious behavior on my part.'

With incredible dexterity the Kid once more brought off the deprecating wave.

'I do not like to speak of it, but I must. Briefly then, I need your protection. I am sure you will respect my confidence, if I tell you why?'

'Sure, miss,' protested the Kid.

Miss Beaumont proceeded.

'Last summer,' she said, 'when I was staying with friends at Newport, I met a gentleman whose name I will not mention. If I did you would recognize it, for he is the son of one of the wealthiest men in the city. We were thrown a great deal in each other's way, and the end of it was that he – he asked me to marry him.'

The Kid murmured sympathetically.

'I thought that I was fond of him,' continued Miss Beaumont, 'and I accepted him. We were engaged secretly. But before either of us could tell our parents, I found out what sort of a man he really was, and I broke off the engagement. He was very violent, and frightened me very much. I am afraid that he is in the habit of drinking a great deal more than is good for him. I did not find that out in time to prevent our engagement, but it was that made me put an end to it. As I said, he was very violent, and refused to accept his dismissal. Fortunately, the house party broke up almost immediately afterward, and I have seen no more of him.

'This morning, however, I received a letter from him. By some means or other, he had got to hear that I was passing through New York and intended to leave by the train I mentioned. In his letter, he says that he is determined to "meet me at the station, to resume," he says, "the discussion we left unfinished at Newport." Now, I must go by that train, for certain reasons which do not matter, and I dare not meet him alone. For a long time I was at my wits' end. I could not think what to do. You see, though my brother has many friends in the city, I am seldom here and have but a few, and they are away just now. And I could not confide in them on such a delicate matter. There is not one of them I could trust not to talk. Now you, Mr Darrell—'

She smiled, and in her smile pathos, compliment, and entreaty were subtly mingled.

'I'll be as silent,' said the Kid, 'as – as Peter Salt, and I couldn't be more than that. But give me his name,' he added fervently. 'I'll give him a jolt that'll settle him for fair. I'm no corker at the game of talk, miss, but when it's the other thing, I'm there with the goods.'

'But above all there must be no scene, except as a last resource. If people heard of it, I think I should die.'

The Kid nodded adherence to this sentiment.

'You must talk to him. All I want is that you come to the station and stay near me in case he – the gentleman I mentioned – is violent.'

'I will,' said the Kid. '*I'll* stop him gettin' gay.'

'He may try to detain me, or, worse still, accompany me on my journey. At all costs, even if you have to employ force, you must prevent that, Mr Darrell.'

'You may leave it,' said the Kid definitely, 'to me, miss.'

'But, unless you are compelled, anything like a scene—'

'I see, miss.'

'Then, good-by. And thank you ever so much. I am more grateful—'

'Proud to be of any service, miss,' said the blushing pugilist.

The Kid was on the platform with commendable punctuality the next morning. Eleven was striking as he turned into the station. He waited till the door opened to admit people to the platform from which the San Francisco train started, and walked up and down like a sentinel, secure in the knowledge that, at any rate, he was first in the field.

Thinking over the matter in the watches of the night, he had come to the conclusion that, as there was every probability of a fracas before twenty-four minutes to twelve, it might be necessary for him, however pure and chivalrous his motives in assaulting a perfect stranger, to vanish without giving explanations and without being recognized. The callous Law which governs assaults and batteries takes no account of Chivalry. It had not failed to occur to him that his position, after the train had borne off his only witness to the excellence of his motive in committing the assault, might be a little equivocal. It might be necessary to trust to rapid flight. For this reason, his 'bubble' waited at the entrance to the station in charge of a boy. Also he had invested a quarter of a dollar in a false mustache. It was becoming, and proved a very effective disguise.

Half an hour passed without the appearance of Miss

Beaumont. The Kid had not expected her to arrive too early. He amused himself in the interim by scanning the passengers as they came up, and endeavoring to detect his man. The half-hour had just struck when a heavily-veiled figure passed him.

'Here I am, miss,' he said.

She started, and dropped a small bag which she carried.

'It's all right, miss. It's me, Darrell. Is he here?'

She had recognized him now, and he saw her smile as she caught sight of the mustache.

'The man in brown,' she whispered, and entered the train.

The Kid was surprised. He had noticed the man in brown. He had been on the platform almost as long as himself, and he, too, had patrolled it in sentinel fashion. But not for a moment had the Kid imagined that this could be his man. Anything more unlike the dissipated young society man – a type which had become familiar to him during his years at Mike Mulroon's – he had never seen. Like all boxers, the Kid judged of a man's condition by the whites of his eyes. An habitual drinker's eyes are not easy to mistake. The whites of this man's eyes were clear and healthy. He had a strong, keen face.

But there was no doubt that he was the right man, for as Miss Beaumont entered the car, he caught sight of her and darted across the now almost empty platform in her direction.

The Kid had taken up his stand opposite the steps, and when the man arrived he found the entrance blocked.

'Excuse me,' said the man, abruptly, but not impolitely.

The Kid did not move.

For the first time the man seemed to scent the partisan.

'Stand aside, you!' he cried.

A rush of steam issued from the funnel of the engine. Belated passengers dashed wildly for seats.

The mouth of the man in brown set like a steel-trap.

'Let me pass!' he hissed. 'I shall not speak again.'

'All aboard! All aboard!' shouted the conductor. 'Step lively there! Step lively!'

The man in brown rapped out a furious oath.

'Out of my way!' he shouted.

The Kid spoke for the first time.

'To the woods!' said the Kid.

Interested faces appeared at the windows of the train.

The Kid stood before the steps of the car in stolid silence.

Suddenly the man darted forward and seized the Kid by the shoulders. The next instant he was lying full length on the asphalt. The Kid was a hard hitter, and righteous indignation had added force to his arm. It would be a quarter of an hour before his enemy could recover from such a blow, on a spot where even a tap is enough to stun.

Even as he fell, the train steamed out of the station.

'This,' thought the Kid, as running figures began to approach from the end of the platform, 'is where I leave for the tall timber!'

Customers at the Kid's saloon during the ensuing week wondered what made the champion so gloomy and disinclined for casual conversation. He seemed to have something on his mind, and once, when Officer Kelly of the police force strode into the bar, he was noticed by the observant to turn a clear shade paler. When Kelly retired after drinking a modest Würzburger, his countenance resumed its normal hue, and he began to talk rapidly, almost incoherently.

The cause of this strange demeanor was a certain 'sensation' of which the papers had made the most during the week. The *Manhattan Daily* had started it, and the other papers had followed in its wake.

It had been heralded by head-lines:

## OUTWITTED

BY A WOMAN

*Gem-Grabber Grace Grant Gets Away.*

DUNN STUNNED

*Detective Dunn Tells How He Was Felled*
*By An Accomplice.*

STILL AT LARGE

*Interview with Detective Dunn*
*'He Was a Tall, Burly Man.'*

That was how the *Manhattan Daily* opened fire.

Having broken it gently, as it were, in this fashion, it went on to describe how Detective Dunn, of the metropolitan force, having received information that Grace Grant, the heroine of the latest New York jewel robbery, was about to make an attempt to leave for California by the morning express, had gone to the station to arrest her. There, however, when on the point of effecting a capture, he had been severely attacked by an accomplice and stunned. The accomplice, said the writer, was being searched for by the police; and it relieved the Kid a little to find that the injured detective described him as a 'tall, burly man with a long black mustache.' His own stature was small, his figure, though sturdy, far from massive, and his long black mustache had gone for ever.

But he passed an unhappy week.

Eight days later a considerate cyclone destroyed most of a small town out West, and Detective Dunn and his troubles ceased to interest the public.

The lane was not wide and the Kid's automobile, which had broken down after the manner of automobiles, blocked a generous two-thirds of it. The greater part of the Kid was out of sight, underneath the machine. The hottest sun that had shone on the State of New York that summer was slowly roasting a pair of brown boots and the lower portion of two flannel-clad legs, which protruded from beneath the wheels. The Kid hated this phase of automobilism, but he went through it conscientiously.

The sound of horses' hoofs mingled with the amateur engineer's murmured imprecations. They slowed down to a walk as they neared the derelict, and finally halted.

'Is there any one in charge of that smoke-wagon?' inquired a voice politely. 'Saved!' he added, 'I see boots. Shop!'

The Kid began to wriggle out from his place of retirement.

'If you can spare me a moment of your valuable time,' continued the horseman, 'I wish you would ease off that bubble a point or two to the left. At present it's taking up most of the road, and this intelligent animal refuses to pass.'

The Kid stood up and inhaled the fresh air.

'Why it's the Kid! I had a sort of idea I'd seen that bubble before. Just the very man I wanted to meet.'

He jumped down from his horse, and approached the Kid with outstretched hand.

'I've been looking for you everywhere. They told me you were in the village. I want a soul-to-soul talk with you when you're through with your tinkering. By the way, you may not remember me. Garth. Tom Garth. I interviewed you for the *Manhattan Daily* when you came to New York after winning the championship. You were in bed. Remember? You got outside your breakfast, while I sat on the chest of drawers and asked you questions. It would have made a good subject for a historical painting. Now do you remember? Don't mind me. We can talk when you've finished. I don't understand bubbles, or I'd help you. As it is, the sun is hot. I have a cigar-case somewhere, and if you look closely you'll see me do my popular imitation of a hard-worked young journalist taking a much-needed rest.'

'Not be long,' responded the Kid, crawling into retreat once more, while Mr Garth, whistling the *Mosquito's Parade* under his breath, sat down by the roadside and felt for his cigars.

Ten minutes elapsed before the Kid, damp and red as to the face, emerged, wiping his hands.

'Done it,' he said complacently.

'Then sit down and have one of these. It's much too hot for the strenuous life. However – Well, Kid, it brings back my vanished youth meeting you like this. Been assaulting the police lately? What's up *now*? I wish you wouldn't spring about like that. It's too hot.'

The Kid continued to gaze at his loquacious companion, in consternation. The lurid episode of Detective Dunn and the female jewel-robber, in whose cause he had displayed so much mistaken chivalry, had begun to fade from his mind, but this sudden, apparently irrelevant, question brought it surging back in all its pristine freshness. How much did the man know?

Mr Tom Garth stretched himself lazily on the grass and blew

a scientific smoke-ring. He was a long, thin young man, with a dark, clever face, and a humorous mouth. He appeared wholly unconcerned at the disturbance he had caused.

'What – what – how? Who's been telling you?' gasped the Kid.

'It's all right,' replied Garth. 'Sit down. It was a shame to spring it on you like that. My passion for the dramatic's quite a disease. You needn't worry. We're all friends here. Nobody but myself knows a word about it. Your cigar's out!'

The Kid subsided to the grass again.

'How did you know?' he asked.

'I recognized you on the platform that day. It was a decent disguise, all the same. I recognized you by your build, and the way you put that shot in at the jaw. Poor old Dunn! Not much need to count ten there. He was out for twenty minutes, and even then he wasn't what you'd call chirpy. I've been wanting to see you ever since, to ask you what the deuce you were at. You're a law-abiding person, I know. Why this sudden outburst of devilry?'

It was with a certain hesitation and confusion that the Kid explained the machinations of the insidious Miss Grant. He had been badly buncoed, and there was not much pleasure to be derived from saying so.

Garth chuckled incessantly throughout the tale. 'Smart girl, that. Deserved to get away. I'm glad she did. Now I'll tell you where I come in. Bear in mind, from this point, a certain proverb you may have heard – one good turn deserves another. I shall come back to it shortly. Well, this was how it was. I know Dunn. He told me he was expecting to make an important arrest at the station. I hovered around to scoop it for my paper. But mark the sequel: I didn't get the scoop I wanted, but I got another twice as good. Have you ever seen an editor smile? You should have seen Taylor's face split in half when I cake-walked into the office with my story. As you know, I put them off the scent by describing you as a burly man. Dunn would have it that his assailant was a fellow about your own build, Kid, but I assured him that he was wrong, and that the jolting he had got had sent his memory off the rails. So that made it all right for you. And the moral of that, as I said before, is, that one good turn deserves another.'

'Anything I can do—' began the Kid fervently.

'Good. I knew you had a noble heart, Kid.

> *I've heard of hearts unkind, kind deeds*
> *With coldness still returning;*
> *Alas; the gratitude of men*
> *Hath oftener left me mourning.*

As one Wordsworth observed. I don't suppose you know him. He held the championship belt for poetry at one time. But he wasn't referring to you. When it comes to gratitude, you're there with the goods. And now I'll tell you what you can do to help me. It's a long story, and I think I'll light another weed before I begin.'

'I'm listening,' said the Kid encouragingly.

Garth lit his cigar, threw the match at the horse, which was still making a hearty meal, and resumed: 'They have an unholy custom in newspaper offices of New York,' he said, 'of dispensing, during the hot weather, with the services of a certain number of their employees. Or, if you want that sentence translated, they bounce about one in every five of the reporters on the papers. There is no animus about it. They hint that you are a splendid fellow, and what the paper will do without you they don't know, but, all the same, would you mind taking a holiday? Thanks, very much. When the summer's over, and people begin to come back to town they take you on again. But in the meanwhile you are at a loose end. That's my case. The *Manhattan Daily* don't want me till the cold weather.'

'It's a burnin' shame!' broke out the sympathetic pugilist.

'Dry the starting tear,' said Garth. 'I don't mind, as far as I'm concerned. In fact, I'm very glad. Being thrifty by nature and habit, I have plenty of money to keep me going till I resume my job. And the holiday is welcome for many reasons, principally because it will give me time to carry out a certain scheme. Whatever you do, try and keep awake now, for this is where you come in.'

The Kid expressed himself all attention.

'I shall now bore you with a little biography. It's painful, but necessary. I was born of poor but honest parents, who sent me to school at an early age, where I met a certain Lord Worfield.'

'A lord!' echoed the interested Kid.

'A lord,' said Garth. 'We were friends at school, and when we went to Oxford we continued friends. In fact, we are still friends. I came out to the States; he stayed at home. Well, Worfield arrived in New York just before I left the paper. He was rolling in money, and showed a pleasant anxiety to get rid of it. After he had seen all the theaters and got tired of all the restaurants, he found – with horror – that he still possessed more than would be good for two men. It was then that he was struck with a bright idea. I hope you're listening. Have another cigar. This was his idea: A thoughtful study of our New York papers had left him with the impression that there was no law of libel in the land; or if there was, that you couldn't say anything about a person bad enough to make a jury give damages. Having got this notion firmly into his head, he came to me.

'"Tom," he said – just like that – "why shouldn't we start a paper that's not only libellous in spots, but all through? The greater the truth the greater the libel. Let's start a weekly that tells the unvarnished truth about all these New York beauties – in Wall Street, and so on. It will sell like hot cakes. And it will be the best rag since Oxford. You shall be editor, and I'll finance the thing."

"Very well," I said, "if you're dying to burn money. But," I added, "we shall want somebody to protect us from infuriated callers. Somebody to sit at the door and throw them downstairs as they arrive. And," I said, "I know the very man – Kid Brady." So there you are, Kid. Will you come in? Handsome pay, and pleasant work. I'll get you fit for your next fight. Join the staff of *Candor* as fighting-editor, and combine business with pleasure.'

'How?' said the Kid. 'I'm not next to the game yet.'

'It's perfectly simple. We want you to be around during office hours to see that strong and angry gentlemen don't come worrying me. I shan't have time to attend to them myself. You will sit in your little rabbit-hutch at the top of the stairs, and when any one calls and asks to see the editor, you will tell him that the editor is not in. If he tries to get past you, it will be up to you to see that he gets the rapid bounce. Don't be violent with them. Simply assist them gently in the direction of the street.'

There was a silence while the idea filtered through into the Kid's brain. Then he rose to a point of order.

'What's going to be doing when they recognize me?' he asked. 'I'd like to help you, Mr Garth, but I daren't risk getting into trouble with the cops. You see, a fighting-man's got to be more careful than most. He don't get let off too easy when he comes into court for hitting people.'

'That's all right, my dear Kid,' said Garth with much cheerfulness, 'don't worry yourself. In the first place, you mustn't hit 'em. I explained that. We don't want New York to be full of Trust Magnates with black eyes. Then a man with your talent for disguise need never be recognized. You shall dress for the part. Doesn't that stir your young blood? We'll get you up as an elderly and respectable partner with a neat gray mustache. Any more objections? He is silent. Ergo, he is convinced. Excellent. All the arrangements are now complete. We shall leave for New York tonight. If you like you can run me down in your bubble. The first number of *Candor* has been ready this many a day. Now that the staff is complete, we can begin. Approach me, Bucephalus, if you have finished your meal. Whoa! And now, Kid,' he added from the saddle, 'get into the bubble, and we'll go back to the hotel and drink success to the paper.'

The Kid had been in some queer situations in the course of his short life, but he was inclined to give the palm to the one in which he now found himself. Every afternoon, Wednesdays and Saturdays excepted, he repaired to his post at the top of the first flight of stairs in the building in which *Candor* rented its offices. Here he sat entrenched behind a wooden barrier, fingering his gray mustache uneasily – the fear that it would come off never left him – and interviewing gentlemen who objected to hearing the truth about themselves. These were of all sorts. On the second day after the appearance of the first number, a tall, somber man in a long fawn-colored dust-coat called. The Kid recognized him from photographs as a celebrated romantic actor.

'I wish to see your editor,' said the great man with ominous calm.

'Editor not in,' replied the Kid glibly.

'You are sure that he is not in?'

'Sure.'

'The better for him,' retorted the other darkly. 'Can you remember a message, my man?'

'Sure.'

'Then give your editor, when he arrives, the compliments of Mr Bodkin, Mr Aubrey Bodkin of the National Theater, and tell him that Mr Bodkin does not lightly forget.'

They were not all so pacific. Arriving one afternoon a little late, the editor of *Candor* had to stand aside on the stairs to allow a procession of two to pass him. The procession was headed by a stout, red-faced gentleman in business suit who moved reluctantly. The rear was brought up by the Kid. He was grasping the visitor by the elbows, and appeared to be supplying the motive force.

'I knew that Wall Street people would be a success,' said Garth to himself with a grin as he watched them disappear.

*Candor* created a considerable sensation from its very first number. Theoretically, New York is empty during the summer; but in practice there are still a few inhabitants. These read the new weekly almost to a man. Its victims bought it from curiosity and against their better judgment. Their friends read it eagerly, amused and interested to find that the truth about the victims had at last become known.

The progress of the paper was like that of a forest fire. Contemporaries in Chicago and St Louis quoted tit-bits from it in their Sunday editions. Astute firms sent in orders for advertisements. Founded to enable Lord Worfield to dispose of his surplus cash with the maximum of amusement to himself, it rapidly began to assume the proportions of a great investment. The expenses were small, the profits large. On the appearance of the eighth number, an attempt was made, by unknown persons, in the absence of the staff, to wreck the office. Garth edited number nine from behind a door with three panels splintered. Number eleven saw his salary doubled, also the Kid's. The Kid had now got well into the swing of his duties, and was enjoying journalism immensely.

One afternoon Garth was writing a trenchant leader, when he was interrupted by a knock at the door.

'Come in,' he cried. 'Hullo, Kid, what's the matter?'

'There's somebody wants to see you,' said the gray-mustached one.

'Tell him I'm not in.'

'It's a lady,' said the Kid with a blushful grin.

Garth clicked with his tongue doubtfully.

'Well,' he said at last, 'show her in. I didn't bargain for this. I wonder what she wants. We haven't had a word about any woman in the paper. There is a line, Kid, and we draw it. Show her in, then. But keep an eye on the stairs and see that no one else gets through.'

The Kid reappeared a moment later, ushering in the visitor. Garth placed a chair for her. She was the type of an American girl who seems to radiate brightness.

'Are you the editor of *Candor*?' she inquired.

'I am,' said Garth. 'Is there anything—?'

'Yes,' she replied decidedly, 'there is. I want you to read this. I'm Julie Weyder, and Cornelius Weyder is my father.'

'I don't need to read the article,' said Garth, 'I think I know the one you mean. It is called *What we think of Mr Cornelius Weyder*, is it not?'

' "Number one." That's it.'

'Exactly. "Number one." H'm. I don't mind admitting to you, Miss Weyder, that this slightly complicates matters. When I – when my contributor wrote that article, he did not take into account the fact that even Copper Kings have those who love them. The consequence was that – er – that, in fact, he rather let himself go.'

'He did,' responded the lady, grimly.

He looked compassionately at her.

'I really do not see what I can do.'

Miss Weyder stamped a minute foot upon the floor.

'Do! You don't see what you can do? Why print a piece next week saying the thing isn't true.'

'I cannot do that, Miss Weyder. I am afraid it is quite true.'

'Well, they ought not to have said it. And I don't believe it's true. And, anyhow, you can deny it in the paper.'

'I am afraid that would scarcely be possible, Miss Weyder. You forget my position as regards the paper. I am a paid servant. If I do not perform my work as my proprietor wishes, I am not doing my duty. My proprietor wishes *Candor* to be run on certain clearly defined lines, and I must do it, however greatly against my will.'

'But you can stop them from printing any more of it. This is number one. How many more are there?'

'It is a series of six,' replied Garth.

'Six! But you must stop them.'

'I am afraid it is impossible. Unless,' he added to himself, 'Worfield will stop the infernal things.'

'Then you're very, very cruel,' said Miss Weyder, her eyes filling with tears.

There was an awkward pause, during which Tom Garth felt more uncomfortable than he remembered ever to have felt before; and then a merciful interruption relieved the tension. The door-handle turned, and Lord Worfield entered.

All three spoke at once.

'Hullo, Tom!' said Lord Worfield.

'Hullo, Jimmy!' said Garth, with fervent gratitude.

'Jimmy!' said Miss Weyder, springing to her feet.

'Why, Julie,' said Lord Worfield, 'I didn't see you. What are you doing here? I was just coming to tell Tom about you. Have you introduced yourselves? This is Tom Garth, Julie. We were at school and Oxford together. Tom, this is Miss Julie Weyder, who has promised to be my wife. We have been engaged since yesterday evening. I was coming to tell you.'

''Gratulate you, old man,' murmured Tom.

'Jimmy, *can't* you do anything? Who is it who owns this paper? Because they have been printing things about father, and it's to be a series of six, and Mr Garth says he has no power to stop it, unless he gets his proprietor's leave. Do you know the proprietor? Can't you speak to him? Look!' She held out a copy of *Candor*. Lord Worfield ran his eye through the article.

'Bitter,' was his comment.

'Smith's stuff is always that,' said Garth eyeing him steadily, 'he thinks the proprietor likes it.'

'So he does,' said Lord Worfield hastily, 'so he does, old chap. Only this is different. You see – I mean – that is to say – What I mean to say is, Mr Weyder being a friend of mine – No, that's not it. I don't know what I'm saying. I didn't know anything about this series. Oh, lord!'

He edged close to Tom.

'For heaven's sake, old chap,' he entreated in a hot whisper, 'don't give me away.'

'Miss Weyder,' said Tom, courteously, 'with your permission, I will change my mind. I will brave my proprietor's wrath and suppress the remaining five articles on my own responsibility.'

The sun broke through the clouds. Miss Weyder dimpled

charmingly, Lord Worfield's long face cleared, and he heaved a sigh of relief, which he instantly changed into a cough.

'Then, that's all right,' he began.

'What is that noise?' inquired Julie.

From the direction of the stairs came the well-known sound of the Kid informing a caller that the editor was not in. Lord Worfield, who was nearest the door, looked out. Then he shut the door with what seemed unnecessary rapidity and decision. His face was pale. From the stairs the sound of shuffling feet made itself heard.

'What is it? Do let me look,' said Julie.

'No, no, it's nothing,' said Lord Worfield, with a ghastly grin. 'It's only that ass of a porter. He often does a sort of dance to keep himself warm.'

Miss Weyder stared.

'To keep himself warm! In a New York summer! I *must* look. The man must be mad.'

'That's just what he is. Just what he is. A little eccentric, that is to say. Tom only engaged him out of charity, because he's old and has a widow and six small children. I mean a wife. That's all.'

The shuffling feet died away. Silence reigned on the stairs.

'Well,' said Julie, 'I must be going. No, you are not to see me home, Jimmy. Good-by, Mr Garth, and thank you so much. I hope your proprietor will not be very angry with you.'

'I don't think he will, Miss Weyder,' said Tom. 'Good-by.'

The door closed behind her.

'My lord!' said Worfield, wiping his forehead with his handkerchief.

'Well, Jimmy,' said Tom Garth, 'so you're hooked at last. No more *Candor* for you after this, I suppose? Candor generally ceases with marriage.'

Lord Worfield breathed heavily.

'The narrowest squeak I ever had,' he said, 'or want to have. Yes, the paper's dead. Do you know who that was that the Kid was showing out just now? Mr Weyder. Julie's father. My lord, what a shave! If she'd seen—! Look here, Tom, I'm awfully sorry to have to put a stopper on the show just when it's beginning to go well, and after all the trouble you've taken; but I simply daren't. If it came out— You don't know old Weyder. It wouldn't take much to make him withdraw his consent.'

'He isn't impressed by the title?'

'Not a bit. And he an American father!'

'I don't know what the world's coming to,' said Tom. 'A man with his dangerous ideas ought not to be at large. Exit *Candor*, then. In life it was beautiful, and in death – RIP.'

'I'm sorry, Tom. Are you – I mean, does this make it at all awkward for you?'

'Don't name it, old man. That's all right. I shall enjoy a holiday, and the *Daily* will take me on again when the cold weather begins. Slay the rag with an easy conscience. You'll be ruining nobody.'

A Trust Magnate met a Wheat King in Wall Street a week later.

'It's dead,' said the magnate.

'What's dead?'

'That filthy rag, *Candor*.'

'Yes, so I see. These papers never last. Good at first, but fall off.'

'Mere flash in the pan,' said the magnate. 'Do we lunch?'

'Kid,' said Tom Garth, as they sat together in the private room in the latter's saloon, 'there never was a good thing on this earth which a woman couldn't smash up in one round, if she started in on it.

> *What mighty ills have not been done by woman!*
> *Who was't betrayed the Capitol? – A woman!*
> *Who lost Mark Antony the world? – A woman!*
> *Who was the cause of a long ten-years' war,*
> *And laid at last old Troy in ashes? – Woman!*

That's poetry, Kid, one Thomas Otway wrote it.'

'He knew his business,' said the light-weight champion of the United States.

The Kid sat in the spring sunlight on the low veranda of the Wheatsheaf Hotel at Green Plains, reading lazily through a copy of a New York evening paper, which had just come in. The tenth page was half-filled with sketches of a humorous nature. He caught sight of his own name, and glanced at them; they were flattering in motive, but candid in detail. They caricatured the Kid, but represented him in the act of performing great feats. One of them pictured certain typical inhabitants of Green Plains coming down from a mountain hut, leading cows and pigs, which, according to the legend beneath, they purposed to wager on the Kid's success in his next fight. In another sketch, Peter Salt was represented flying through the air on receiving one of the champion's scientific drives.

'Up at Green Plains,' said the paper, 'there is a man who will own the whole town if he wins his next fight. His name is Kid Brady, and to the inhabitants of that noble joint there is not a bigger man in the world. He went up there the other day to train for his fight with Jimmy Garvis, which takes place at Philadelphia on the 14th; and now every man, woman, and child for miles around talks about him. Between whiles the Kid takes photographs with his nice new snap-shotter. As views of representatives of American beauty, his photographs of Mike

Mulroon and Peter Salt have Burr Intosh beat to a standstill every time.'

In short, the Kid was on active service again, and glad to be there. His old opponent, Jimmy Garvis, had been very busy of late. He had fought two fights, and won both with ease; and the public began to talk about a return match with the Kid. The champion was delighted to meet them half-way.

So Jimmy Garvis threw down his glove, and the Kid picked it up with alacrity. The two met in the most friendly fashion at dinner at a sporting restaurant, and signed the articles. A 'play or pay' match, either party not putting in an appearance in the ring to forfeit his money, and the loser to get a proportion of the purse. Having settled these weighty matters, the pair shook hands, and parted, Jimmy Garvis to Atlantic City, the Kid to his favorite Green Plains.

He loved to train at Green Plains. The writer of the newspaper report had added picturesque touches here and there, but in the main his statements were correct. Green Plains was fond and proud of the Kid, and was backing his chances at Philadelphia with more than it could afford to lose with any comfort. Whenever the Kid walked abroad in the village, groups of graybearded, slouch-hatted farmers rallied around to inquire after his health. Later, they usually retired to drink it.

They were certainly justified in risking their belongings on the champion's chances. The Kid had one very important advantage over a great many of his rivals. He did not drink. In or out of training, he touched no alcohol of any description. On one occasion a hearty person, who had come all the way from Denver to see him, burst into his saloon with a cheery 'What's yours, Mr Brady?' The Kid had ordered a lithia water, and the man from Denver was nearly a fortnight getting over the shock of it. Jimmy

Garvis, on the other hand, was in the habit of running loose when not in training. Fur coats and cigars a foot long were Jimmy's simple pleasures, together with divers 'small bottles.' The consequence was that he needed stricter handling than the Kid when a fight was in preparation. The Kid's training was merely a development of his everyday life.

Mike Mulroon was charmed with his man's progress. As he explained volubly to Peter Salt every evening when the Kid had gone to bed, the boy trained himself. He never showed signs of even wanting to do the things which he ought not to do. He abandoned smoking without a murmur. He took Peter Salt's hardest blows with unruffled cheerfulness. He never lost his appetite. Twelve miles go-as-you-please along the country roads never wearied him. His conversation, though there was not much of it – he was never garrulous when training had once begun seriously – was bright. He never lay awake at nights. And now, two days before the battle, he was down to the prescribed weight, and as full of life as a kitten. What was not steel was india-rubber.

'Kid,' said Mike Mulroon, as he rubbed him down after his brine bath, 'yer a fool. An archangel couldn't have trained better. Faith, afther ye've put Jimmy to sleep, ye'll have to give an exhibition spar, or the people will be afther complainin' that they have not had the worth of their money. It won't go into a second round.'

And even Peter Salt had been moved from his wonted silence, and had congratulated the Kid in measured speech.

The Kid dropped the paper beside his chair, and looked around about him. The grass-grown square was empty. The veranda was empty. A sudden desire came over him to talk to some one. Mike and Peter had gone for a stroll through the town.

There was nobody near. But as he looked down the road, he was aware of a man walking in the direction of the hotel. His eyes lit up as he perceived that the man carried a camera. The Kid had only recently been bitten by the craze for taking photographs, and he was at the stage where the victim's chief pleasure is to foregather with another victim, and talk camera to him.

The man paused opposite the veranda, and fanned himself with his handkerchief. When he removed his hat, the Kid saw that he had gray hair.

'Good afternoon,' said the man.

'Afternoon,' said the Kid.

'Can you tell me where I can find Mr Brady?'

'My name.'

'Then may I ask you,' said the man with a friendly smile, 'if you would mind sitting there while I take a photograph of you?'

'Sure,' replied the Kid. 'I take photographs.'

'So I saw in the papers. I must show you my camera when I have taken you. It's a new make. Now! Thank you, thank you. Poof! This is warm weather, sir, for the time of year.' The Kid agreed. The man entered the veranda and drew a chair up beside the champion's. The next moment their heads were close together, inspecting the camera, which was of a new make.

The Kid noticed that his friend kept shooting sharp glances at him from time to time, as he explained the mechanism of his camera. Frequently he would catch his eye, and on such occasions he always detected something searching in his gaze, as though he were trying to read some secret there. It might have been a mere mannerism, but it embarrassed the Kid. The man with the camera quickly showed that there was method in what he did. He turned to the Kid with some abruptness.

'You will excuse me, sir,' he said, 'but are you aware that there is something decidedly wrong with your eyes?'

The Kid stared.

'My eyes?' he repeated. 'What's the matter with them?'

'If you want the technical term,' said the man, 'it's amblyopia.'

'What's that?' said the Kid.

'It is an affection of the eyes. In your case very pronounced. I wonder you have not noticed it yourself.'

'My eyes are the best ever. I can see anything.'

'That, I fear, signifies nothing. There is such a thing as seeing too well. Do your eyes get tired easily?'

'Never.'

'Headaches ever?'

'Not one. Not when I'm in training,' he added.

The man caught him up at once.

'Ah, then you do have them when you're out of training? How often?'

'Twice a year,' hazarded the Kid.

The man shook his head.

'Bad,' he muttered, 'bad. I think I see now. You smoke when not in training?'

'Sure.'

'But knock it off when you have a fight on hand?'

'Sure.'

'Now I understand. You have tobacco amblyopia. I don't know how much you smoke; but a man with your eyes ought never to have smoked at all. I am surprised that you have had no trouble with them before this. I attribute it to the fact that you are continually leaving off smoking for long periods at a time. That has acted as a check on the disease.'

'But what is it? Can't it be cured?'

'That I cannot tell you from a cursory examination. I should say with care, yes. But I cannot say for certain unless I test your eyes carefully. Have you ever been to an oculist?'

'Never.'

'You should have gone. Well, fortunately, I am an oculist by profession myself. You may have heard my name? Theodore Shaw, of Boston. No? Well, well, it shows one how purely local a reputation of my kind is. If you wish it, I will examine your eyes, Mr Brady. I cannot do it very thoroughly, of course; but it may enable me to give you some advice which will be valuable to you. Shall we go into the hotel?'

What followed was Greek to the Kid. In a little room at the back of the hotel Mr Shaw put him through a series of what seemed to him meaningless maneuvers, asked him a good many apparently irrelevant questions, held a candle before his eyes, shook his head a great many times, and finally led him out into the sunlight once more.

'Well?' queried the Kid anxiously.

'The disease,' said the man slowly, as one who weighs his words, 'has not gone too far. It can be cured. But you must be careful. Very careful. No more smoking, I need hardly say.'

'Not another cigar,' said the Kid fervently, 'if Teddy Roosevelt offered it me himself.'

'You must take great care not to strain the eyes.'

'You bet I will.'

'And there is another thing. And I am afraid,' added the man, 'that this puts you in a very difficult position.'

'Yes,' said the Kid.

'It is this. In their present condition any blow, even the slightest, would have a very injurious effect on your eyes.'

The Kid's jaw fell. He looked blankly at the speaker.

'Yes,' he went on, 'a tap would injure them. A really severe blow would almost certainly destroy your eyesight altogether. I understand that in a few days you are to fight the ex-champion at Philadelphia. Well, I can only say that it will be suicidal for you to attempt any such thing. I am sincerely sorry for you; but it is necessary that you should know the truth before it is too late. It was providential that I happened to come here this afternoon.'

The Kid sat staring across the square with unseeing eyes. He hardly heard what was being said to him. A drummer drove past in his cart, and shouted a cheerful greeting to him. He returned it mechanically. There seemed to be a weight on his brain which deprived him of the power of thinking.

He became aware that his companion was bidding him good-by. He caught some remark about a train. He stood up, and shook hands, scarcely knowing what he did.

'And if you will take my advice,' the stranger concluded, 'you will make arrangements at once for withdrawing from this fight. It is a large sum to forfeit; but what is it in comparison with sight?'

'But if I don't fight ... the bets! They're bettin' on me everywhere. If I quit, every one who has bet on me will lose their money.'

'That is true. But even that is surely not worth considering. Think of it. Think what blindness means! At your age! Well, I must go. Good-by again. I shall leave you to think it over.'

And the last the Kid saw of the man from Boston was the tail of his coat disappearing rapidly around the corner of the square, as he hurried off to the station.

The Kid sat on, thinking. His brain was clearer now, and

he could weigh matters better. On the one hand, there was blindness. He shut his eyes, and tried to realize what this meant. Everlasting darkness. And all because he had done what every other man he had ever met had done. It was hard. Mike would be back soon. He would tell him everything, and the fight would be canceled. But the thought of Mike brought back to him the reverse side of the picture. Play or pay. Fight or forfeit. Mike, he knew, had betted heavily on him, as he always did. He could not sell him. And the thousands who had done the same. He could not sell them. There were farmers at Green Plains who had wagered their savings on him. It was his duty to go through with his contract. He could not draw back now. And yet . . .

Fumbling in his pocket, his fingers came in contact with a coin. An idea struck him, and he drew it out. Play or pay? Sudden death . . .

The coin spun up in the eye of the sun, and rolled across the white, dusty road. It was a nickel. If it fell with the V uppermost – no, with the head – no, the V – He wavered, undecided. Then he pulled himself together. The V it should be. If the head was underneath, he would fight.

His heart was beating fast, as he stepped into the road.

Half-way across he came upon it, almost buried in the dust.

It was the V.


'Mike,' said the Kid next day, 'I think I won't put the gloves on with Peter. I've had enough sparring. I'll take it out with the bag.'

'Very well, Kid,' said Mulroon. 'Ye're a quare boy with yer fancies. But yer down to the weight, so it don't matter.'


A volley of shouts came from all corners of the hall as the ex-champion's right glove neatly passed the Kid's guard, and left an angry red mark on his side. There was a brief rally, and the fighters clinched.

'Get a move on, Jimmy,' cried a voice from near the door, 'it's all your own.'

'Clever, Kid; box clever!' This in the accent of New York.

'Silence there during the rounds.'

'Break away,' said the referee curtly, walking between the two men. Their arms relaxed their hold, and they stepped back a pace. The Kid had a swift sight of his antagonist's flushed face as he dashed in in his hurricane style. His left flashed out, and met empty air; he was conscious of a great, but curiously vague, shock. Something seemed to snap at the back of his head.

A face appeared beside him, working violently. He recognized it as Mike Mulroon's. He wondered idly why there should be no more of Mike but a head and shoulders. Then it struck him that he was lying on the stage. His eye was caught by a movement in the air above him. A man in evening dress was standing by his side, sawing rhythmically with his right arm. There was a great deal of noise. He heard his own name shouted. Some one was telling him to get up. Mike again. Why did Mike want him to get up? He felt very comfortable where he was; though something made it difficult for him to think coherently. Somebody was counting. He could just hear him through the din – 'Seven ... Eight.' Then he realized.

The next moment the roar of the audience changed to a crescendo. The Kid was up again. Staggering, but on his feet. Hope still remained.

Jimmy Garvis, waiting with every muscle tense on the other side of the ring, sprang forward like a tiger to complete the work his cross-counter had begun. Instinct told the Kid to slip, and he was in the middle of the ring, with his opponent turning back to press him again. Another slip. This time he was by the ropes.

As his opponent rushed, there came from behind him the penetrating sound of a gong, and the applause broke out again. The third round was over.

'Where's your three to two now?' said the Californian by the door triumphantly to his neighbor. The other, whose home was New York, did not reply. He was beginning to wish, like many others present that night, that he had kept his dollars safely in his pocket instead of wagering them on the champion. The Kid was filling his supporters with consternation. From the first round he had fought like a novice. All the dash and fire which had won him the championship were missing. His attitude was strained and awkward. His leads were hesitating, ineffective. If he had not been Kid Brady, whose gameness it was absurd to question, one would have said that he was afraid. And so he was. For the first time in his life, the Kid knew what fear meant. He was sick with the terror of receiving his opponent's hurricane swings in his eyes. All his thoughts were concentrated on saving them. And so far he had been successful. But like a cold hand on his heart the thought haunted him that it could not last. Sooner or later the fatal blow must get through.

It happened before the fourth round had been in progress for thirty seconds. Jimmy Garvis feinted, drew the Kid's counter, and got home heavily. The Kid staggered back on the ropes, with lights dancing before his eyes. Another second, and they had cleared. But the mischief was done.

And now there came over him a complete revulsion of feeling. The worst had happened. The suspense was over. He was conscious of no sensation other than of icy rage. He forgot that he was boxing for a prize. His opponent seemed to him inhuman, some relentless devil maliciously intent on destroying him. There was a moment's pause, while the two sparred for an opening; and then the Kid went in with a vicious fury which made this fight a topic of conversation for years afterward in the smoking-rooms of Philadelphia and New York. There was no staying such an onslaught. Twice the ex-champion fell, to rise gallant, but weak, to renew the contest. He reeled across the ring like a rudderless derelict. Every one was standing up now. It was plain that the end must come soon.

For the third time the Californian went to the floor. The Kid, standing over him, was forced back to the farther side of the ring. The referee's hand rose and fell. A dead silence had gripped the spectators, and the referee's voice sounded thin and clear as he counted out the ten seconds of grace.

'Six ... Seven.'

Jimmy Garvis struggled to his knees. His gloved hand wandered out and clutched the ropes.

'Eight ... Nine.'

The hand relaxed, and he sank to the boards again.

'Ten,' said the referee, and waved his arm toward the Kid.

'Take me away, Mike,' said the Kid. 'I must see an oculist.'

'Brady,' said the oculist. 'Not Kid Brady, the champion?'

'I'm Kid Brady. Look at my eyes. Is there any hope?'

'While there is beefsteak,' said the oculist solemnly, 'there is always hope. But it is certainly a very fine black eye. You've come to the wrong man, my boy. You should have gone to a butcher.'

'Will I go blind?'

The oculist looked at him curiously, and patted him on the shoulder.

'You're unstrung, my boy. I don't wonder, if you've come

straight from a championship fight. Sit down and rest a while. It will soon pass off.'

'I've got tobacco am – amblyopia,' said the Kid, 'and I'm going blind. He said a hard blow would do it.'

'He. Who is he? And what do you know of amblyopia? But I'll look at your eyes, if that will set your mind at rest. Now.' He rose, and turned on an electric light. 'Sit down. Now look straight here where I am pointing. That's right. Don't move.'

A light flashed into the Kid's eyes. The oculist was examining them through a small glass. Twice the light flashed, and then the oculist laid down the glass.

'Amblyopia!' he said. 'You've no more got amblyopia' – he looked around him for a suitable simile – 'than the table,' he added.

'How on earth do you get these ideas into your head? My dear boy, don't do that! Bear up.'

For under the strain of the fight and the fright and the relief of it all the Kid's nerves had given way suddenly and completely, and he was sobbing like a child.

'Drink this,' said the oculist briefly. The Kid broke through his principles, and felt the better for it.

'Now, let me hear all about this. Who has been telling you that your eyes were wrong?'

'Dr Shaw.'

'And who in the name of all the saints you have never heard of is Dr Shaw?'

'Dr Theodore Shaw, of Boston. A famous oculist.'

'Famous, is he?' said the other drily. He fumbled among the books on the table, and produced a red-backed volume. 'Just glance through the S's in this book, and if you find your friend Shaw there I'll give you as many dollars as you won tonight.'

'It's not there,' said the Kid, having searched.

'So I imagined. That book contains the names of all the oculists, known and unknown, in the country. You would think a famous man like Dr Theodore Shaw, of Boston, would be there, wouldn't you?'

The Kid looked dazed.

'But—?' he began.

'My dear boy,' said the oculist, 'I don't know very much about the modern ring, but I do know that people bet on fights. And when people bet, there are apt to be shady tricks. If you cannot see now that this was a low dodge to induce you to give up the fight, you are blinder even than Dr Theodore Shaw prophesied that you would be.'

Then the Kid saw.

His voice trembled when next he spoke. 'If I could find him—' he said, clenching his fists and breathing heavily.

'There was once,' said the oculist sententiously, 'an optimistic gentleman who tried to find a needle in a haystack. He did not succeed.'

His first impression was that he had been knocked out and was slowly recovering from the effect of the blow – all the symptoms were there – the dull, dazed feeling at the back of the head, the sickness, and the curious sense of being separated by a great gulf from the things of this world. He opened his eyes, half expecting to see the dismayed face of Mike Mulroon bending over him. He found himself looking at what appeared to be a wooden ceiling less than a foot above his head. And as he looked the whole of his world seemed to give a violent lurch, righting itself a moment later only to repeat the performance with a greater emphasis, and the feeling of nausea which had lain hitherto vaguely at the back of his consciousness grew suddenly till all other emotions faded before it, and he realized at last that he was in a ship and out at sea.

Then memory came back to him. He had gone to San Francisco to box at the Mechanics' Pavilion. A heavy-weight of fame had fallen on lean days, and a monster benefit had been organized by his admirers. The Kid had sparred three rounds with an English middle-weight who had crossed the Atlantic in search of international laurels.

After going through this exhibition to the great gratification of the audience, he had changed his clothes and started out to see a little of the town. A polite stranger, who had scraped acquaintance with him in a cigar store, had offered his services as a guide. The Kid had accepted them. The stranger seemed a pleasant sort of man, cheerful and anxious to make himself agreeable; and they had got on very well together until a sudden and powerful blow on the head had made the Kid unable to appreciate the society of any man, however cheerful. Between this incident and his awakening on board the ship there was a hiatus. What had happened to him during that period and how long that period might have been he did not know.

As a matter of fact, things had fallen out after this fashion: The blow which had put the light-weight champion of America out of business had been administered – by means of a sand-bag – by a bosom friend of the cheerful stranger. Thereafter the Kid, chloroformed by way of preventing all accidents, had been put on board a boat and rowed out to the ship on which he now was.

As he stood clutching at the side of his bunk, and wishing faintly that he could die more quickly than he seemed to be do-ing, there appeared, framed in the hatchway above him, a head and shoulders.

'Hello, sonny,' said the visitor.

The Kid made no reply. He was in no fit condition for small talk.

'Got over it, then?' said the other, who was apparently deter-mined to make conversation. 'Crimes! You were mighty snug, you bet you were. Wish I'd had half of what put you to sleep, sonny. Some boys gets all the luck that's coming to them.'

The Kid clutched his support in silence. At that moment the head and shoulders were removed from the hatchway, leaving a square of gray, cloudy sky, and from above another voice made itself heard. 'Where the devil's that young mongler that came aboard last night?'

A murmur from the owner of the head and shoulders.

'Down below, is he? Fancies he's a passenger perhaps? Wants his cup of tea took him. I shouldn't wonder. Here, let me come.' Another head and shoulders appeared in the hatchway. The newcomer, to judge from the half of him which was visible, seemed to be muscular – his shoulders were broad and heavy, and bad-tempered, – his eyes spoke eloquently as he glared down at the Kid.

After a brief inspection he proceeded to supplement the language of the eyes with the spoken word.

His opening remarks consisted mainly of oaths. The Kid, his eyes glued firmly on the opposite wall, made no reply. He was but dimly aware that he was being addressed. He was acutely conscious of feeling very ill. Everything else, including the angry man, who was now climbing down the ladder, was unreal and unsubstantial.

'Now, then,' said the man, stepping off the last rung; 'get a move on you, you young mongler. Get busy. On deck with you! You aren't on Telegraph Hill now, and don't you forget it.'

The Kid spoke for the first time.

'In – a – minute,' he groaned.

And simultaneously things began to happen. Dazed and help-less, he found himself in an incredibly short space of time roughly but skillfully kicked up the ladder and on the deck, where a knot of men had collected in an unostentatious manner to observe his arrival. On the appearance of the Kid's aggressor, the group broke up with the unanimity of a chorus in an opera, and began to work energetically at anything that came to hand. The Kid lay where he had fallen, to receive a second measure of kicks.

The pain dissipated the clouds that were over his mind and even achieved a momentary triumph over the seasickness. He staggered to his feet and put his hands up.

'Talking back, are you?' said his persecutor. 'If it's fight you want—'

The Kid was too weak to ward off his bull rush. A smashing blow on the chest sent him across the deck.

'And now,' said the other, two minutes later; 'you get busy and help the cook. That's what you're fit for. Cooky!'

'Sir?' said a polite voice.

'None of your damned airs, cooky! Take this man and give him something to do. You get in there sharp, or I'll have a word or two with you. I'll show you who's mate on this ship.'

With all the fight knocked out of him, the Kid went meekly across to the galley. 'Take a seat,' said the cook. 'You'll feel better soon. Rough man, the mate. Here, take these potatoes and begin peeling 'em. You'd better seem to be doing something useful in case he looks in.'

The rough handling he had received had not dulled the Kid's senses so much that he could not recognize the voice as that of a gentleman. Through all the complicated and unpleasant sensations from which he was suffering at the moment he was conscious of a certain surprise at finding such a man in such a place. There was something in the voice which reminded him of Tom Garth and Lord Worfield.

'If you will allow me to give you a word of advice,' continued the cook, as the Kid sat down and began upon the potatoes, 'I should recommend you to lie low while you're on this ship. It is what they call a hell ship, in these parts, which means that the officers give the men hell whenever they see a chance. I noticed just now that you showed fight. I shouldn't do that again. There is nothing our genial Snow dislikes so much. I have seen him handle men far worse than he handled you because they would show fight. Much better take what he gives you philosophically. And if you work hard, you'll miss a lot of it. He's a brute, but he mostly confines his attentions to the shirkers. By Jove, I really beg your pardon. I've been preaching a regular sermon. Sorry if I've bored you. How do those potatoes progress?'

The Kid was staring into vacancy.

'I'll lay for him,' he said between his teeth.

'My dear man, don't be an idiot. Can't you see that all the cards are against you? You can't call a policeman here. There aren't any police on the *May Moon*. I wish there were. We could do with a few. You take my tip, and lie low.'

'He kicked me,' muttered the Kid, half to himself. 'I've got it in against him, and he's going to get it good.'

'Look here,' said the cook, 'do be sensible. I know you must feel rather raw about it, but do be reasonable. I'm sorry for you, and I shouldn't care to see you get into any more trouble. You obviously can't fight the man.'

'Why not?' asked the Kid, looking up quickly. 'Would he use a gun?'

'No,' said the cook, 'I don't suppose he'd use a gun, but he'd use his hands. You'd have a fair enough fight, if I know him; but where would you be? You'd be giving away at least three stone. It won't do. Be sensible. And, for goodness sake, hurry up with those potatoes, or there won't be any dinner for anybody.'

The Kid relapsed into silence again.

His seasickness wore off. The following day was calmer, as far as the ocean was concerned. As regarded the mate, heavy weather was still the order of the day. With his companions in the fore-castle he got on amicably. In a rough way they seemed sorry for him, though it was plain that they regarded him as a fool for having allowed himself to be shanghaied. It was only Snow, the mate, who rendered life unhappy. The other officers of the ship, including the captain, seemed from what he saw of them to be mild in comparison. The captain, in particular, was reputed to be a 'white' man. But he was apt to concentrate his attention on the handling of the vessel. The driving of the crew he left almost entirely to Snow.

During the days in which he was occupied in getting his sea-legs the Kid made the further acquaintance of the refined Cooky, and learned many things from him. He learned the technicalities of the new little world in which he found himself, why people did what they did with various ropes, what was meant by 'forrard,' which side of the vessel was port and which starboard. Few ships can have included in their crew so complete a land-lubber as the Kid. He was a lost sheep in the wilderness. He was a stranger among a people speaking strange tongues. It was hopeless to think of making a sailor of him by blows or explanations; and there fell to him, in consequence, the menial tasks which some-body has got to do, even on board ship. At the end of a couple of days, he found himself, fit and well once more, with a sort of roving commission to make himself generally useful. His duties were varied and extensive, and nobody seemed able to fix any definite limit to them. He waited on the captain and the mates in the cabin, scrubbed the decks, kept an occasional watch, and on one occasion did able-bodied seaman 'Lefty' Rawson an excellent turn by keeping him below when he wished to go on deck.

Mr Rawson contrived, on coming aboard, to bring with him a square bottle of the strongest whiskey he could purchase in the whole length of the San Francisco waterside; on the second day out he drank this, neat, in a series of long and exhaustive gulps, immediately after which he expressed a desire to go on deck and ascertain – by means of personal research – the exact color of the mate's interior. It was as he reached the foot of the companion ladder that the Kid intervened.

The subsequent proceedings took place on the forecastle floor, to the great gratification of able-bodied seaman Jake Burt, who surveyed the scene from his bunk, and offered between the puffs of his pipe shrewd advice to the combatants. The fight was not lengthy. Mr Rawson, directing his entire attention to strangling the Kid, left that expert free to hook him with both hands on the point of the jaw, and presently Lefty's head fell back on the boards with a crack, and the Kid went upstairs to attend to his other duties.

The incident did him a great deal of good in forecastle circles. Restored to sense and sobriety once more, Mr Rawson was gratitude itself. He offered, moreover, first-hand evidence of the Kid's powers in a rough and tumble.

'Sure it's little I remember,' he said handsomely that night, 'me bein', as you may say, not meself, what with the whiskey and the pleasurable excitement of it all; but I will say this, that I've not been handled so neatly since I miscalled Long Jack Harvey a liar in Sweet's rathskeller in New Orleans ... And him a boy!' he added, gazing fondly at the Kid.

Mr Burt also gave his testimony.

'As good as a play, it was,' said he happily. 'There was me in me bunk, and me friend Lefty on the floor yellin' to beat the band and me brave boy on top of him feelin' for his jaw left and right, as if it was all a stage play and me having paid for a front seat in the orchestra chairs. It's me that 'ud wish to see him go through the performance with the mate doing me friend Lefty's part.'

'And me, too,' said one of the other men. The Kid sprang to his feet and banged the table with his fist. This sudden gust of popularity had swept away the wall of sullen resignation which he had built up as a protection against the company into which he had been forced. His eyes shone. For the moment he was in much the same condition as Lefty Rawson had been earlier in the day.

'And so you shall,' he cried; 'I'm laying for him. He kicked me, the—'

There was a cheer, half encouraging, half ironical, from the other occupants of the forecastle. He was proceeding, when a quiet voice at his elbow stopped him.

'Chuck it, my dear man, chuck it,' said the interrupter.

It was Cooky, calm and well-bred as ever, and as he looked at him the Kid's bombast died away. It occurred to him that he was making a fool of himself. 'Anyway, I will,' he concluded weakly. The cook went on smoking in silence.

The Kid found an opportunity next day of speaking to the friendly Burt, whom he had recognized as the man who had been the first on board to speak to him.

'Who's Cooky?' replied Burt to his question. 'Sure there's many of us would like to know that. He's the great mystery, is Cooky. You can see he's not one of the boys, not one of us. He's a Britisher is Cooky, and an educated man, too. That's what Cooky is. And what he's doing roasting meat for sailor-men is more than I can tell you, me son. Gone wild, likely, and had to skip from home. Like many another young bhoy who didn't know what was good for him. Dad, I was a farmer's boy in the old country meself once. Whist, here's the mate!'

Snow had come up as they were talking. He glared at the Kid. Much had to be done, in his opinion, before the latter's education as a unit of the company of the *May Moon* could be considered complete; and he was always on the look-out for a chance to further this education.

'You lazy young hound,' he said, twisting him around by his shoulder and kicking him toward the galley, 'go and help the cook. Get busy now, before I set about you.'

The Kid made no resistance. He added mentally another mark to the mate's account. Things were working up for the storm; but the moment was not yet.

The cook was in the galley, whistling plaintively to himself.

'See here,' said the Kid, when he had got to work; 'I want to ask you something.'

'Yes.'

'When you came on this ship, what did that mate do to you?'

'Much the same as he has been doing to you.'

'What! Kicked you?'

'Frequently.'

'And what did you do?'

'I did nothing.'

'And why doesn't he do it now?'

'He gets tired of it, I suppose. I believe the man feels it a sort of holy duty to make every new hand's life a hell to him for the first few days, just as a sort of formal welcome aboard, making him free of the ship, as it were. After that the new man gets to be one of the many, and only comes in for the amount of handling that every one gets.'

'But you don't,' said the Kid. 'What did you do to get quit of him?'

The cook chuckled.

'Mine was rather an exceptional case. On the third day out on my first voyage he got annoyed with me – I forget why – and kicked me so energetically that I was laid up for four days, unable to move. As there was nobody else on board who knew the first word about cooking, the ship's company lived for those four days on half-raw meat and biscuits. They all got very bad inside, and I believe there was nearly a mutiny. Since then he has left me alone. He would like to jump on me, but he's scared; "letting 'I dare not' wait upon 'I would.'" But I'm afraid you can't expect such an exemption. Your best plan is to lie low. You'll be all right soon. Lie low.'

'And be kicked?'

'And, if you must, be kicked.'

'You'll see,' said the Kid. 'Next time he touches me—'

The cook looked bored. Like most Englishmen of good birth and a public-school education, he had a strong objection to the type of person who utters wild threats which he cannot possibly carry into effect.

'You're not Mr James J Jeffries, by any chance?' he inquired.

The Kid, missing the irony, was merely surprised at this ignorance on the part of one who in other respects was intelligent beyond the ordinary.

'Jim's a heavy-weight,' he said.

'You talk big enough to be one,' retorted the other. 'Perhaps you're Jimmy Garvis, then?'

'Jimmy!' said the Kid with scorn; 'I can whip Jimmy all right, every time.'

He was not usually prone to flap his wings over a defeated rival, but the cook's words had touched a tender spot.

'You – what?' said the cook, dropping a plate. 'You whipped Jimmy Garvis? Then who the deuce are you?'

'Brady's my fighting name, Kid Brady. But my real name's Darrell.'

'Kid Brady!'

The cook swayed with laughter.

'We mustn't keep this to ourselves,' he said; 'I'll tell the boys tonight.'

In the forecastle that night the Kid listened, blushing, to Mr Burt's stately speech of welcome. The crew of the *May Moon*, according to Mr Burt, were proud to be in the same room with such a mighty man of his hands.

'Didn't I tell ye,' said Mr Lefty Lawson, when he had finished, 'that this was no orrdinary boy. He handled me beautiful. Beautiful!'

'Mr Brady,' said the cook, in his quiet voice, 'if you purpose to interview the mate at any time, as you suggested, you will carry with you the good wishes of this meeting. We have all suffered.'

It seemed to the Kid that the moment had come, that there was nothing to be gained by delay. He had grown used to the motion of the ship by this time, and the sea air made him feel particularly ready for work. He had been in good condition before leaving San Francisco, and now he felt fit to fight for his title of Champion of America. He kept a watchful eye on the mate as he went about his duties. It was for Snow to give the signal for combat. He must not be the aggressor. The rules of discipline on board the *May Moon* were curious, but rigid. If a man attacked his superior officer, it was mutiny, and he suffered for it. But if the officer attacked him, he was at liberty to defend himself, always provided that he considered the game worth the candle. In this case rank was waived for the moment, the pair met as man to man, fought the thing out, and, when satisfied, resumed their respective positions. The captain was supposed to be officially ignorant of the episode.

It was a curious custom and might not have suited another

ship, but on the *May Moon* it had existed since the vessel's launching. As a rule, especially since Snow had come into power, the crew were content to take matters quietly instead of giving battle. The mates of the *May Moon* had always been men of thews, and a fight would seldom have been satisfactory to the aggrieved seamen. Legend spoke of a certain Billy Priest, who in the dim past had fought a mate and knocked him clean over the side of the ship, subsequently diving after him and saving his life. But Billy Priest had passed beyond the ken of man and left no successor. There had not been a genuine fight on the *May Moon* for half a dozen voyages.

The Kid watched the mate, and the crew watched the Kid. There was a quiet over the ship which might have struck an observer as ominous. Men found themselves talking in whispers. There was trouble in the air.

It broke on the second day after the meeting in the forecastle, quite suddenly. The Kid was carrying a bowl of potatoes to the galley. The ship was moving at three-quarter speed over a calm sea. Just as he reached the galley the vessel heeled, slightly, but enough to make him stumble. As he recovered himself a stream of potatoes jumped across the deck. He stooped to pick them up, and was struck while in that position by a massive boot. He looked up.

The mate was standing over him.

The Kid rose with a grin. He was conscious of that curiously tense, happy feeling which always came to him when the gong gave him the signal to leave his corner. And on this occasion it was supplemented by a definite thrill of anger. In the ring he missed this exhilarating thrill.

'Clumsy young devil,' said the mate; 'pick 'em up. Get busy. Pick 'em up.'

The world seemed to pause for a moment. All movement appeared suddenly suspended. Forward a knot of men were standing silent spectators. Cooky had come out of his galley with a dish in his hand, and was watching the Kid with a suspicion of a smile. The Kid's eyes were fixed on the mate's face.

Then in a flash the latter's expression changed. Comprehension came into his eyes, and his mouth curled in a sneer.

'It's that, is it?' he said softly. 'You – young—'

And then the spell was broken, everything was activity once more, and the battle had begun.

To the spectators the mate's rush seemed as swift as it was savage; but a man who has fought and beaten the best light-weights in the ring has his own ideas of speed. To the Kid there was something ludicrously clumsy in the onslaught of this bull of a man. He had side-stepped and hooked thrice to the body before his adversary's blow had well exhausted itself. The mate did not turn easily on the slippery deck, and the Kid's right was home on his ear before he had faced around. He shook his head furiously, and charged forward again. The straightest left in America stopped him as completely as if he had met a bullet. Never in his life had the Kid hit so quick and hard. The thought of all that he had suffered from this man lashed him to a cold viciousness. Even now he was aching from that kick he had received among the potatoes. Four times his left went out like a stone from a sling, and a hum of applause rose from the knot of men by the forecastle as the mate, staggering under the third blow, reeled and went down beneath the fourth. The Kid drew back and waited. He was cooler than he had ever been before in a fight. He felt that he could go on all day. He was giving away fifty pounds and three inches of height. It seemed nothing to him.

The mate was no quitter. He was up again in a couple of seconds, and boring in as before. Blow after blow went home; but he came up for more, and forced the Kid toward the side. Here space was less, and weight would begin to tell. The Kid saw this, and knew that he must end the business soon or be cornered. Twice he swung his right to the other man's jaw, but Snow's iron muscle saved him from going out. The Kid shot in his right once more. The mate's head went back with a jerk, and the Kid side-stepped. As he did so he trod on one of the potatoes he had spilt. His ankle half turned under him, and he fell. He was up again and in position in a moment, but there was no danger. Snow was lying on his face, one arm outstretched, the other doubled beneath him. The last blow had completed the work of the other two. His man was down and out.

A shout went up from the group by the forecastle. The Kid found his right hand being shaken.

'Exit Goliath,' said the quiet voice of Cooky. 'Come and have a wash and brush-up, David, my son!'

The Kid was look-out man that night. A fine day had been succeeded by stars and a clear sky. The water looked oily, almost solid. The Kid was not sentimental by nature, but a feeling of deep content possessed him as he watched. It was worth being shanghaied to get such a night as this on the open seas.

Into the ray of a lantern, there loomed a huge shadow.

'Is that the boy from San Francisco?'

The Kid recognized the voice of the mate, and kept a wary eye on him.

'Yes, sir,' he said.

The mate lit his pipe, and puffed in silence for some minutes.

'Not so darned poor,' said the mate at length, jerking the stem of his pipe toward the star-powdered sea.

'Fine,' agreed the Kid.

There was another long silence.

'See here,' growled the mate, sucking furiously at his pipe at intervals, as if what he was saying was difficult to say; 'see here, it's up to me to say just this . . . I don't – in a manner of speaking . . . do any darned climbing down as a general thing . . . But I'm a man that knows when he's met a tougher proposition than himself.'

He removed his pipe and tapped it against the side of the ship.

'And it's up to me to say you're it. I never thought a boy could put me out of business. But you've done it, and that's all there is about it.'

He paused again.

'Don't know what you are when you're ashore, but what I say's this. You ought to be a fighter. Take it up. You'd make money at it. That's what I say.'

'Well, I have,' said the Kid with a grin.

'What, you a fighter?'

'That's it.'

'Yes?'

'I fight at the light-weight limit,' said the Kid simply, 'and I'm the Champion of the States.'

'Kid Brady!'

'That's me.'

The huge form of the mate lurched into the light. His voice when he spoke had an animation which it had lacked before. 'Say, this is the best thing I've heard this trip! See here, it's no pie to be put to sleep by a boy not big enough to look over the side of a ship; but a light-weight champeen's a thing that might happen to any one. See, here, Mister Brady, you and me's got to be friends, sure. I'm rough in my ways, but I'm a man what recognizes talent. I'm proud to meet you, Mister Brady. Shake.'

He extended a hand.

'Why, sure,' said the Kid, taking it.

THE END

# A Man of Means

# CONTENTS

When a seed-merchant of cautious disposition and an eye to the main chance receives from an eminent firm of jam-manufacturers an extremely large order for clover-seed, his emotions are mixed. Joy may be said to predominate, but with the joy comes also uncertainty. Are these people, he asks himself, proposing to set up as farmers on a large scale, or do they merely want the seed to give verisimilitude to their otherwise bald and unconvincing raspberry jam? On the solution of this problem depends the important matter of price, for, obviously, you can charge a fraudulent jam-disseminator in a manner which an honest farmer would resent.

This was the problem which was furrowing the brow of Mr Julian Fineberg, of Bury St Edwards, one sunny morning when Roland Bleke knocked at his door; and such was its difficulty that only at the nineteenth knock did Mr Fineberg raise his head.

'Come in – that blamed woodpecker out there!' he shouted, for it was his habit to express himself with a generous strength towards the junior members of his staff.

The young man who entered looked exactly like a second clerk in a provincial seed-merchant's office – which, strangely enough, he chanced to be. His chief characteristic was an intense ordinariness. He was a young man; and when you had said that of him you had said everything. There was nothing which you would have noticed about him, except the fact that there was nothing to notice. His age was twenty-two, and his name was Roland Bleke.

'Please, sir, it's about my salary.'

Mr Fineberg, at the word, drew himself together much as a British square at Waterloo must have drawn itself together at the sight of a squadron of cuirassiers.

'Salary!' he cried. 'What about it? What's the matter with it? You get it, don't you?'

'Yes, sir, but—'

'Well?'

'It's too much.'

Mr Fineberg's brain reeled. It was improbable that the millennium could have arrived with a jerk; on the other hand, he had distinctly heard one of his clerks complain that his salary was too large. He pinched himself.

'Say that again,' he said.

'If you could see your way to reduce it, sir—'

It occurred to Mr Fineberg for one instant that his subordinate was endeavouring to be humorous, but a glance at Roland's face dispelled the idea.

'Why do you want it reduced?'

'Please, sir, I'm going to be married.'

'What the devil do you mean?'

'When my salary reaches a hundred and fifty, sir. And it's a hundred and forty now, so if you could see your way to knocking off ten pounds—'

Mr Fineberg saw light. He was a married man himself.

'My boy,' he said, genially, 'I quite understand. But I can do you better than that. It's no use doing this sort of thing in a small way. From now on your salary is a hundred and ten. No, no, don't thank me. You're an excellent clerk, and it's a pleasure to me to reward merit when I find it. Close the door after you.'

And Mr Fineberg returned with a lighter heart to the great clover-seed problem.

The circumstances which had led Roland to approach his employer may be briefly recounted. Since joining the staff of Mr Fineberg he had lodged at the house of a Mr Coppin, in honourable employment as porter at the local railway station. The Coppin family, excluding domestic pets, consisted of Mr Coppin, a kindly and garrulous gentleman of sixty; Mrs Coppin, a somewhat negative personality, most of whose life was devoted to cooking and washing up in her underground lair; brothers Frank and Percy, gentlemen of leisure, popularly supposed to be engaged in the mysterious occupation known as 'lookin' about for somethin''; and, lastly, Muriel.

For some months after his arrival Muriel had been to Roland Bleke a mere automaton, a something outside himself that was made for neatly-laid breakfast-tables and silent removal of plates at dinner. Gradually, however, when his natural shyness was soothed by use sufficiently to enable him to look at her when she came into the room, he discovered that she was a strikingly pretty girl, bounded to the north by a mass of auburn hair and to the south by small and shapely feet. She also possessed what we are informed – we are children in these matters ourselves – is known as the R.S.V.P. eye. This eye had met Roland's one evening as he chumped his chop; and, before he knew what he was doing, he had remarked that it had been a fine day. From that moment matters had developed at an incredible speed. Roland had a nice sense of the social proprieties, and he could not bring himself to ignore a girl with whom he had once exchanged easy conversation about the weather. Whenever she came to lay his table he felt bound to say something. Not being an experienced gagger, he found it more and more difficult each evening to hit on something bright; until, finally, from sheer lack of inspiration, he kissed her.

If matters had progressed rapidly before, they went like lightning then. It was as if he had touched a spring or pressed a button, setting vast machinery in motion. Even as he reeled back, stunned at his audacity, the room became suddenly full of Coppins of every variety known to science. Through a mist he was aware of Mrs Coppin crying in a corner, of Mr Coppin drinking his health in the remains of his sparkling limado, of brothers Frank and Percy, one on each side, trying to borrow simultaneous half-crowns, and of Muriel, flushed but demure, making bread pellets and throwing them in an abstracted way, one by one, at the Coppin cat, which had wandered in on the chance of fish.

Out of the chaos, as he stood looking at them with his mouth open, came the word 'banns,' and smote him like a blast of east wind.

It is not necessary to trace in detail Roland's mental processes from that moment till the day when he applied to Mr Fineberg for a reduction of salary. It is enough to say that for quite a month he was extraordinarily happy. To a man who has had no experience of women, to be engaged is an intoxicating experience, and at first life was one long golden glow to Roland. Secretly, like all mild men, he had always nourished a desire to be esteemed a nut by his fellow-men; and his engagement satisfied that desire. It was pleasant to hear brothers Frank and Percy cough knowingly when he came in. It was pleasant to walk abroad with a girl like Muriel in the capacity of the accepted wooer. Above all, it was pleasant to sit holding Muriel's hand and watching the ill-concealed efforts of Mr Albert Potter to hide his mortification. Albert was a mechanic in the motor-works round the corner, and hitherto Roland had always felt something of a worm in his presence. Albert was so infernally strong and silent and efficient. He could dissect a car and put it together again. He could drive through the thickest traffic. He could sit silent in company without having his silence attributed to shyness or imbecility. But – he could not get engaged to Muriel Coppin. That was reserved for Roland Bleke, the nut, the dasher, the young man of affairs. It was all very well being able to tell a sparking plug from a commutator at sight, but when it came to a contest in an affair of the heart with a man like Roland, Albert was in his proper place, third at the Pole.

Probably, if he could have gone on merely being engaged, Roland would never have wearied of the experience. But the word 'marriage' began to creep more and more into the family conversation, and suddenly panic descended upon Roland Bleke.

All his life he had had a horror of definite appointments. An invitation to tea a week ahead had been enough to poison life for him. He was one of those young men whose souls revolt at the thought of planning out any definite step. He could do things on the spur of the moment, but plans made him lose his nerve.

By the end of the month his whole being was crying out to him in agonized tones, 'Get me out of this! Do anything you like, but get me out of this frightful marriage business!'

If anything had been needed to emphasize his desire for free-dom, the attitude of Frank and Percy would have supplied it. Every day they made it clearer that the man who married Muriel would be no stranger to them. It would be his pleasing task to support them, too, in the style to which they had become accustomed. They conveyed the idea that they went with Muriel as a sort of bonus.

The Coppin family were at high tea when Roland reached home. There was a general stir of interest as he entered the room, for it was known that he had left that morning with the intention of approaching Mr Fineberg on the important matter of a rise in salary. Mr Coppin removed his saucer of tea from his lips. Frank brushed the tail of a sardine from the corner of his mouth. Percy ate his haddock in an undertone. Albert Potter, who was present, glowered silently.

Roland shook his head with the nearest approach to gloom which his rejoicing heart would permit.

'I'm afraid I've bad news.'

Mrs Coppin burst into tears, her invariable practice in any crisis. Albert Potter's face relaxed into something resembling a smile.

'He won't give you your rise?'

Roland sighed.

'He's reduced me.'

'Reduced you!'

'Yes. Times are bad just at present, so he has had to lower me to a hundred and ten.'

The collected jaws of the family fell as one jaw. Muriel herself seemed to be bearing the blow with fortitude, but the rest were stunned. Frank and Percy might have been posing for a picture of men who had lost their fountain pens.

Beneath the table the hand of Albert Potter found the hand of Muriel Coppin, and held it; and Muriel, we regret to add, turned and bestowed upon Albert a half-smile of tender understanding.

'I suppose,' said Roland, 'we couldn't get married on a hundred and ten?'

'No,' said Percy.

'No,' said Frank.

'No,' said Albert Potter.

They all spoke decidedly, but Albert the most decidedly of the three.

'Then,' said Roland, regretfully, 'I'm afraid we must wait.'

It seemed to be the general verdict that they must wait. Muriel said she thought they must wait. Albert Potter, whose opinion no one had asked, was quite certain that they must wait. Mrs Coppin, between sobs, moaned that it would be best to wait. Frank and Percy, morosely devouring bread and jam, said they supposed they would have to wait. And, to end a painful scene, Roland drifted silently from the room and went upstairs to his own quarters.

There was a telegram on the mantelpiece.

'Some fellows,' he soliloquized happily, as he opened it, 'wouldn't have been able to manage a little thing like that. They would have given themselves away. They would—'

The contents of the telegram demanded his attention.

For some time they conveyed nothing to him. The thing might have been written in Hindustani.

It would have been quite appropriate if it had been, for it was from the promoters of the Calcutta Sweep, and it informed him that as the holder of ticket number 108,694, he had drawn Gelatine, and in recognition of this fact a cheque for five hundred pounds would be forwarded to him in due course.

Roland's first feeling was one of pure bewilderment. As far as he could recollect, he had never had any dealings whatsoever with these open-handed gentlemen. Then Memory opened her flood-gates and swept him back to a morning ages ago, so it seemed to him, when Mr Fineberg's eldest son Ralph, passing through the office on his way to borrow money from his father, had offered him, for ten shillings down, a piece of cardboard, at the same time saying something about a sweep. Partly from a vague desire to keep in with the Fineberg clan, but principally because it struck him as rather a doggish thing to do, Roland had passed over the ten shillings; and there, as far as he had known, the matter had ended.

And now, after all this time, that simple action had borne fruit in the shape of Gelatine and a cheque for five hundred pounds.

Roland's next emotion was triumph. The sudden entry of cheques for five hundred pounds into a man's life are apt to produce this result.

For the space of some minutes he gloated; and then reaction set in. Five hundred pounds meant marriage with Muriel.

His brain worked quickly. He must conceal this thing. With trembling fingers he felt for his match-box, struck a match, and burnt the telegram to ashes. Then, feeling a little better, he sat down to think the whole matter over.

His meditations brought a certain amount of balm. After all, he felt, the thing could quite easily be kept a secret. He would receive the cheque in due course, as stated, and he would bicycle over to the neighbouring town of Lexingham and start a banking account with it. Nobody would know, and life would go on as before.

He went to bed and slept peacefully.

It was about a week after this that he was roused out of a deep sleep at eight o'clock in the morning to find his room full of Coppins. Mr Coppin was there in a nightshirt and his official trousers. Mrs Coppin was there, weeping softly, in a brown dressing-gown. Modesty had apparently kept Muriel from the gathering, but brothers Frank and Percy stood at his bedside, shaking him by the shoulders and shouting. Mr Coppin thrust a newspaper at him as he sat up, blinking.

These epic moments are best related swiftly. Roland took the paper and the first thing that met his sleepy eye and effectually drove the sleep from it was this headline:

### ROMANCE OF THE CALCUTTA SWEEPSTAKE

And beneath it another:

### POOR CLERK WINS £40,000

His own name leaped at him from the printed page. And with it that of the faithful Gelatine.

Flight. That was the master-word which rang in Roland's brain as day followed day. The wild desire of the trapped animal to be anywhere except just where he was had come upon him. He was past the stage when conscience could have kept him to his obligations. He had ceased to think of anything or anyone but himself. All he asked of Fate was to remove him from Bury St Edwards on any terms.

It may be that some inkling of his state of mind was wafted telepathically to Frank and Percy, for it cannot be denied that their behaviour at this juncture was more than a little reminiscent of the police force. Perhaps it was simply their natural anxiety to keep an eye on what they already considered their own private gold-mine that made them so adhesive. Certainly there was no hour of the day when one or the other was not in Roland's imme-diate neighbourhood. Their vigilance even extended to the night hours, and once, when Roland, having tossed sleeplessly on his bed, got up at two in the morning, with the wild idea of stealing out of the house and walking to London, a door opened as he reached the top of the stairs, and a voice asked him what he thought he was doing. The statement that he was walking in his sleep was accepted, but coldly.

It was shortly after this that, having by dint of extraordinary strategy eluded the brothers and reached the railway station, Roland, with his ticket to London in his pocket and the express already entering the station, was engaged in conversation by old Mr Coppin, who appeared from nowhere to denounce the German Emperor in a speech that lasted until the tail-lights of the train had vanished and brothers Frank and Percy arrived, panting.

A man has only a certain capacity for battling with Fate. After this last episode Roland gave in. Not even the exquisite agony of hearing himself described in church as a bachelor of this parish, with the grim addition that this was for the second time of asking, could stir him to a fresh dash for liberty.

Although the shadow of the future occupied Roland's mind almost to the exclusion of everything else, he was still capable of suffering a certain amount of additional torment from the present; and one of the things which made the present a source of misery to him was the fact that he was expected to behave more like a mad millionaire than a sober young man with a knowledge of the value of money. His mind, trained from infancy to a decent respect for the pence, had not yet adjusted itself to the possession of large means; and the open-handed *rôle* forced upon him by the family appalled him.

When the Coppins wanted anything they asked for it; and it seemed to Roland that they wanted pretty nearly everything. If Mr Coppin had reached his present age without the assistance of a gold watch, he might surely have struggled along to the end on gun-metal. In any case, a man of his years should have been thinking of higher things than mere gauds and trinkets. A like criticism applied to Mrs Coppin's demand for a silk petticoat, which struck Roland as simply indecent. Frank and Percy took theirs mostly in specie. It was Muriel who struck the worst blow by insisting on a hired motor-car.

Roland hated motor-cars, especially when they were driven by Albert Potter, as this one was. Albert, that strong, silent man, had but one way of expressing his emotions – namely, to open the throttle and shave the paint off tram-cars. Disappointed love was giving Albert a good deal of discomfort at this time, and he found it made him feel better to go round corners on two wheels. As Muriel sat next to him on these expeditions, Roland squashing into the tonneau with Frank and Percy, his torments were subtle. He was not given a chance to forget, and the only way in which he could obtain a momentary diminution of the agony was to increase the speed to sixty miles an hour.

It was in this fashion that they journeyed to the neighbouring town of Lexingham to see M. Etienne Feriaud perform his feat of looping the loop in his aeroplane.

It was brother Frank's idea that they should make up a party to go and see M. Feriaud. Frank's was one of those generous, unspoiled natures which never grow *blasé* at the sight of a fellow-human taking a sporting chance of *hari-kari*. He was a well-known figure at every wild animal exhibition within a radius of fifty miles, and M. Feriaud drew him like a magnet.

'The blighter goes up,' he explained, as he conducted the party into the arena, 'and then he stands on his head and goes round in circles. I've seen pictures of it.'

It appeared that M. Feriaud did even more than this. Posters round the ground advertised the fact that, on receipt of five pounds, he would take up a passenger with him. To date, however, there appeared to have been no rush on the part of the canny inhabitants of Lexingham to avail themselves of this chance of a breath of fresh air. M. Feriaud, a small man with a chubby and amiable face, wandered about signing picture-postcards and smoking an unlighted cigarette, looking a little disappointed.

Albert Potter was scornful.

'Lot of rabbits,' he said. 'Where's their pluck? And I suppose they call themselves Englishmen. I'd go up precious quick if I had a five-pound note. Disgrace, I call it, letting a Frenchman have the laugh of us.'

It was a long speech for Mr Potter, and it drew a look of respectful tenderness from Muriel.

'You're so brave, Mr Potter,' she said.

Whether it was the slight emphasis which she put on the first word, or whether it was sheer generosity that impelled him, one cannot say; but Roland produced the required sum even while she spoke. He offered it to his rival.

Mr Potter started, turned a little pale, then drew himself up and waved the note aside.

'I take no favours,' he said, with dignity.

There was a pause.

'Why don't *you* do it?' said Albert, nastily. 'Five pounds is nothing to you.'

'Why should I?'

'Ah! Why should you?'

It would be useless to assert that Mr Potter's tone was friendly. It stung Roland. It seemed to him that Muriel was looking at him in an unpleasantly contemptuous manner. In some curious fashion, without doing anything to merit it, he had apparently become an object of contempt and derision to the party.

'All right, then, I will,' he said, suddenly.

'Easy enough to talk,' said Albert.

Roland strode with a pale face to the spot where M. Feriaud, beaming politely, was signing a picture-postcard.

Some feeling of compunction appeared to come to Muriel at the eleventh hour.

'Don't let him,' she cried.

But brother Frank was made of sterner stuff. This was precisely the sort of thing which, in his opinion, made for a jolly afternoon. For years he had been waiting for something of this kind. He was experiencing that pleasant thrill which comes to a certain type of person when the victim of a murder in the morning paper is an acquaintance of theirs.

'What are you talking about?' he said. 'There's no danger – at least, not much. He might easily come down all right. Besides, he wants to. What do you want to go interfering for?'

Roland returned. The negotiations with the bird-man had lasted a little longer than one would have expected. But then, of course, M. Feriaud was a foreigner, and Roland's French was not fluent.

He took Muriel's hand.

'Goodbye,' he said.

He shook hands with the rest of the party, even with Albert Potter. It struck Frank that he was making too much fuss over a trifle, and, worse, delaying the start of the proceedings.

'What's it all about?' he demanded. 'You go on as if we were never going to see you again.'

'You never know.'

'It's as safe as being in bed.'

'But still, in case we never meet again—'

'Oh, well,' said brother Frank, and took the outstretched hand.

\*   \*   \*

The little party stood and watched as the aeroplane moved swiftly along the ground, rose, and soared into the air. Higher and higher it rose, till the occupants were invisible.

'Now,' said brother Frank. 'Now watch. Now he's going to loop the loop.'

But the wheels of the aeroplane still pointed to the ground. It grew smaller and smaller. It was a mere speck.

'What the dickens—?'

Far away to the west something showed up against the blue of the sky – something that might have been a bird, a toy kite, or an aeroplane travelling rapidly into the sunset.

Four pairs of eyes followed it in rapt silence.

It was a delightful sunny morning in mid-July, and Dermot Windleband, sitting with his wife at breakfast on the veranda which overlooked the rolling lawns and leafy woods of his charming Sussex home, was enjoying it to the full. His Napoleonic features (his features were like that because he was a Napoleon of Finance) were relaxed in a placid half-smile of lazy contentment; and his wife (who liked to act sometimes as his secretary) found it difficult to get him to pay any attention to his morning mail.

Mrs Windleband liked to act sometimes as her husband's secretary, because it recalled old times. In point of fact she had once been his secretary. Dermot had married her, with the least possible delay, on discovering that she had provided herself with a duplicate key to his safe and was in the habit, during his absence, of going very thoroughly through his private papers.

Almost all financiers of anything like real eminence marry their secretaries. It is, on the whole, cheaper to keep a wife who knows all one's secrets than to pay the salary which a secretary who happened to know them would demand.

'There's an article here, in the *Financial Argus*, of which you really must take notice,' Mrs Windleband gently insisted. 'It's most abusive. It's about the Wildcat Reef. They assert that there never was any gold in the mine and that you knew that perfectly well when you floated the company.' She put down the paper for a moment and looked inquiringly at her husband. 'That's not true, is it? You had the usual mining expert's report, didn't you?'

'Of course we had. Very satisfactory report, too. Unfortunately the fellow who wrote it depended rather on the ineradicable optimism of his nature than on any examination of the mine. As a matter of fact he never went near it.'

Mrs Windleband whistled.

'That's rather awkward. The *Argus* say that they have sent out an expert of their own to make inquiries, and hope to have his report for publication within the next fortnight. What are you going to do about it?'

'Nothing,' replied Dermot, with a yawn. 'And, to save you the trouble of wading any farther through that mass of dreary correspondence, I may inform you that, for the future, I propose to do nothing about everything.'

'Dermot!'

Her husband went on placidly:

'Not to put too fine a point on it, dear Heart-of-Gold, the gaff is blown – the game is up. The Napoleon of Finance is about to meet his Waterloo.'

'Surely things are not as bad as all that?'

'They're worse. I'm absolutely up against it this time.'

The failure to lay his hands upon so pitiful a sum as twenty thousand pounds was, he proceeded to explain to his wondering wife, to be the cause of his undoing. Twenty thousand pounds had to be found within the next fortnight, or – they would have to book their passages to the dear old Argentine.

'But twenty thousand pounds!' objected Mrs Windleband,

incredulously; 'you *must* be able to get that. Why, it's a mere fleabite.'

'On paper – in the form of shares, script, bonds, promissory notes – twenty thousand pounds is, I grant you, a fleabite. But when the sum has to be produced in the raw in flat, hard lumps of gold, then it begins to assume the proportions of a bite from a hippopotamus. I can't raise it, dear Moon-of-my-Desire, and that's all about it. So there we are; or, to put it more accurately, here we shall very shortly not be. The Old Guard, Josephine, have failed to rally round their beloved Emperor; so – St Helena for Napoleon.'

Although Dermot Windleband described himself as a Napoleon of Finance, a Cinquevalli of Finance would, perhaps, have been the more accurate description. As a juggler with other people's money Dermot was emphatically the Great and Only. And yet his method – like the methods of all Great and Onlies – was, when one came to examine it, simple in the extreme. Say, for instance, that the Home-Grown Tobacco Trust – founded by Dermot in a moment of *ennui* – failed, for some inexplicable reason, to yield those profits which the glowing prospectus had led all and sundry to expect; Dermot would appease the angry shareholders by giving them preference shares (interest guaranteed) in the Sea-Gold Extraction Company, hastily floated to meet the emergency. When the interest became due it would, as likely as not, be paid out of the capital just subscribed for the King Solomon's Mines Exploitation Company, the little deficiency in the latter being replaced in its turn, when absolutely necessary and not before – by the transfer of some portion of the capital just raised for yet another company. And so on, *ad infinitum*. It was more like the Mad Hatter's tea-party than anything else.

The only flaw in Dermot's otherwise excellent method was that he could never stop and take a rest. He had to keep on all the time floating new companies to keep the existing ones afloat. Sometimes, in his more optimistic moments, he cherished a wild hope that he would succeed one day in floating a company that would, by some fluke, pay its way, and so give him a chance to catch up with himself; but the day, somehow, never seemed to arrive. He had solved the problem of Perpetual Promotion, and had to suffer the consequences of his own ingenuity.

On the whole, it was rather a relief than otherwise to Dermot to discover that the game was up. He had had about enough of it. Still, he objected to the manner of his defeat. Twenty thousand pounds ought not to have caused the fall of one who had in his time handled millions – even if most of those millions were only on paper. Twenty thousand pounds was not enough. The amount was not Napoleonic. It ought to have been two hundred thousand pounds at the very least. The ignominious character of the defeat that stared him in the face was the one factor that inclined Dermot to go on with the fight, if by any possibility it could be managed.

'Are you absolutely sure, Dermot, that nothing can be done?' persisted Mrs Windleband, doggedly. 'Have you tried everyone?'

'Everyone – the Possibles, the Probables, the Might-be-Touched, and even the Highly-Unlikelies. Never an echo came to the minstrel's wooing song. No, my dear; we've got to take to the boats this time, and that right soon. Unless, of course, some-one possessed at one and the same time of twenty thousand pounds and a very confiding nature, happens to tumble out of the sky.'

As the words left his lips an aeroplane came sailing over the tops of the trees that lay below them. Gracefully as any bird it came down on the lawn not twenty yards from where the Windlebands were seated.

'Who is the intrepid aviator?' queried Dermot, lazily, as a nimble little figure, clad in overalls, hopped from the machine and helped out his companion, whose clumsy progress to earth was rather that of the landsman getting out of an open boat in which he has spent a long and perilous night at sea. 'Looks like one of those French chaps.'

'Doesn't matter a bit who the intrepid aviator is,' rejoined Mrs Windleband, in a voice that shook with unwonted excitement. 'It's the other man that I'm interested in. Don't you see who it is? That's Roland Bleke.'

'Roland Bleke?' The Napoleon of Finance shook his head. The name seemed to convey nothing to him.

'Yes, yes – Roland Bleke!' repeated Mrs Windleband, impatiently. 'My dear, you must have heard of him. The man who won the Calcutta Sweep and was kidnapped, or something, at Lexingham yesterday by that French aviator – what's his name? – Etienne Feriaud. The papers are full of it this morning.'

'Ah, I haven't read the papers this morning. Hence my ignorance on the score of Mr Roland Bleke. The world knows nothing of its greatest men. How on earth did you recognize the chap?'

'From his picture, of course.'

She pointed to a photograph which adorned the front page of one of the illustrated dailies that lay on the table before them. Dermot glanced at it, and then said, admiringly, to his wife:

'What a wonderful woman you are! I couldn't have done that. You must get the gift from your uncle.'

Mrs Windleband's uncle was one of those learned professors who can recognize a giant mastodon from a shin-bone dug out of an African swamp.

'I think,' said Mrs Windleband, 'that we ought to go and see what we can do for Mr Bleke.'

'I don't,' rejoined her husband, decidedly. 'They've torn up our croquet lawn with that infernal machine of theirs. My instincts are all against stirring a finger on Mr Bleke's behalf.'

His wife stared at him in astonishment.

'Are you quite well, dear?' she asked, in an anxious tone. 'You don't seem to understand. Roland Bleke netted forty thousand pounds when he won the Calcutta Sweep. That was only a little more than a month ago. From what they say of him in the papers – it seems he's only a seed merchant's clerk in some small provincial town – he can't have spent it all yet. He wouldn't know how.'

A light began to dawn upon her husband. He rose quickly from his chair. The old fighting spirit asserted itself once more. Napoleon was himself again. Waterloo might yet be averted.

' "You made me love you – I didn't want to do it," ' he hummed, inconsequently. 'But, by gum, if ever a man married the right woman it was my father's only son. Come along, old girl. You're quite right. The commonest instincts of humanity demand that we should go to the assistance of this unfortunate Mr Bleke.'

When they got down to where the aeroplane was lying they found the little man in overalls busy tinkering at the engine. His companion was watching the operation in a helpless sort of way, and the Windlebands noticed that, in spite of the heat of the morning, he was shivering violently.

'Not had an accident, I hope, Mr Bleke?' inquired Dermot, pleasantly.

Roland Bleke turned and looked at him with watery, lacklustre eyes. Roland was being kept too busy, by one of the worst colds of the century, to have time to wonder, even, how this stranger came to know his name.

'Doe; doe accident, thag you,' he replied, miserably, as he blew his nose. 'Somethig's gone wrog; but it's not very serious, I'm afraig.'

M. Feriaud, having by this time adjusted the defect in his engine, rose to his feet and bowed to the Windlebands.

'Excuse if we come down on your lawn,' he said, apologetically, 'but we do not trespass long. See, *mon ami*,' he turned, radiant, to Roland, 'everything OK now. We go on.'

'No,' said Roland, very decidedly.

'*Hein?* What you mean – No?'

'I mean that I'm not going on.'

A shade of alarm clouded M. Feriaud's weather-beaten features. The eminent birdman did not wish to part with Roland. Towards Roland he felt like a brother. Roland had notions about payment for little aeroplane flights which bordered on princely.

'But you cannot give up now,' he objected, almost tearfully. 'You say, "Take me to France wis you—"'

'Daresay I did,' admitted Roland. 'But it's all off now; see? Rather than trust myself again in that machine of yours I'd—'

What it was that he would rather do than trust himself again to the aeroplane Roland Bleke, for some reason, elected not to divulge; but his manner gave one to understand that it would be something considerable.

'But it is not fair! It is all wrong!' protested M. Feriaud, turning with an aggrieved air of appeal to the Windlebands, and gesticulating freely in illustration of his wrongs. 'He give me one hundred pounds to take him away from Lexingham. Good. It is here.' He slapped his breast pocket. 'But the other two hundred pounds which he promise to pay me when I land him safe across the Shannel – where is zat?' He took Roland by the arm. 'No, no, *mon ami*; business are business. You must come wis me.'

Roland broke away from the birdman's clutch.

'I will give you,' he said hastily getting out his pocket-book, 'two hundred and fifty pounds to leave me safe where I am.'

A smile of brotherly forgiveness lit up M. Feriaud's face. The generous Gallic nature asserted itself. He held out his arms affectionately to Roland.

'Ah – now you talk!' he cried, in his impetuous way. '*Embrassez-moi, mon cher!* You are fine shap.'

Roland escaped the proffered embrace by busying himself with counting out the bank-notes which he had taken from his case.

Roland heaved a sigh of relief when, five minutes later, the aeroplane rose dizzily into the air and flew away in the direction of the sea; then he indulged in a series of sneezes that made the welkin ring.

'You're not well, you know,' said Dermot, looking at him critically.

'I've caught a slide cold, I fadcy,' said Roland, accompanying the remark with a trumpet *obbligato* on his handkerchief. 'You see, we've been flying about more or less all night – that French ass lost his bearings – and my suit is a bit thin. But I'm all right.'

'You're not all right, my dear boy,' insisted Mrs Windleband, with an air of almost motherly solicitude. 'You ought to be in bed.'

'Perhaps you're right,' admitted Roland, looking helplessly round, as though he expected to see a bed somewhere on the surrounding lawn. 'Can you tell me if there is an hotel anywhere near?'

'Hotel? I'm not going to let a man in your condition go to any hotel,' announced Dermot, in his big-hearted way, taking Roland, as he spoke, firmly by the arm. 'You're coming right into my house and up to bed this instant minute.'

Roland's first instinct, when he discovered that the Good Samaritan who had taken him in was no less a personage than the great Dermot Windleband, was to struggle out of bed and make his escape, even though the effort were to cost him his life. Dermot Windleband was a name which Roland, during his mercantile career, had learned to hold in something closely approaching to reverence – as that of one of the mightiest business brains of our time. Even old Fineberg, whose opinion of humanity at large was unflattering in the extreme, accorded to Dermot Windleband a sort of grudging admiration.

To have to meet so eminent a person in the capacity of an invalid – a nuisance about the house – made Roland long for a rapidly fatal termination to his illness. The kindnesses of the Windlebands – and there seemed to be nothing that they were not ready to do for him – worried him almost into his grave. When Mrs Windleband came into the room in which he lay and, with her own hands, poured out his medicine and put his bed straight, and then sat down and read to him, Roland suffered tortures of embarrassment. Mrs Windleband was an angel, he admitted that; but angels' visits, to a man of retiring disposition, are apt to be trying. He felt even worse when the great Dermot himself came up to the sick-room and sprawled genially over the bed, chatting away just as if he were an ordinary human being and not one of the Master-Minds of the Century. Roland wanted to hide his head under the bed-clothes, so unworthy did he feel of this high honour.

How he came to tell the Windlebands all about the unfortunate matter of Muriel Coppin, Roland never quite knew; but he did. They were very sympathetic. Mrs Windleband said she could see clearly that Muriel was a designing young woman, from whom Roland was quite right to run away. The great

Dermot was of the same opinion, but added that he feared his spirited action was going to cost Roland a bit.

'Tell you what I'll do,' said Dermot, after thinking over the situation for a while, 'I'll send my own lawyer down to her with, say, one thousand pounds – not a cheque, understand, but one thousand golden sovereigns that he can *show* her – roll about on the table in front of her eyes. Very few people of that class can resist money when they see it in the raw. She'll probably jump at the thousand and you'll be out of your trouble.'

'I'd rather make it two thousand,' said Roland. He had never loved Muriel Coppin, and the idea of marrying her had been a sort of nightmare to him, but he wanted to retreat with honour.

'Very well, make it two, if you like,' assented Dermot, indifferently; 'though I don't quite know how old Harrison is going to carry all that money.'

As a matter of fact, old Harrison never had to try. On thinking it over (after he had cashed Roland's cheque) Dermot came to the conclusion that seven hundred pounds would be quite as much money as it would be good for Miss Coppin to have all at once; and so it was with seven hundred sovereigns only that old Harrison was sent out on his errand of temptation. As Dermot had foreseen, the sight of the virgin gold was too much for Miss Coppin. She jumped at it.

Roland, man-like, was a little disappointed when he heard that Muriel had agreed to settle. Glad as he was to escape marrying her, he did feel that she ought to have demanded higher compensation than a beggarly two thousand pounds for his loss. He hinted this to Dermot. In the circumstances Dermot did the right – the tactful thing. He forbore from hurting his guest's feelings still further by enlightening him to the fact that Miss Coppin had been quite content to accept a market valuation of her lost lover which amounted to little more than a third of that sum.

Roland was able to sit up and take nourishment – nay, to come down to the dining-room and take nourishment in large quantities – before the Napoleon of Finance began the real campaign.

Dermot selected with care the right strategic moment at which to strike the first blow. It was after dinner – and a remarkably good dinner at that – a dinner at which the wines had been of the choicest and the liqueurs perfection. Roland's experience of dinners at which the wines were of the choicest and the liqueurs perfection was strictly limited. Moreover, during the period of convalescence from influenza few men are at the height of their alertness. Consequently, the conditions were highly favourable – from the Napoleonic point of view.

'You know, Bleke, I've taken a great fancy to you,' said Dermot, suddenly, as they sat smoking together, after Mrs Windleband had left the room.

Roland blushed with gratification. His private estimate of himself was, he felt, at last being justified. The Coppins hadn't thought much of him; Muriel had patently preferred a mere mechanic; old Fineberg had treated him more or less as dirt; but, by Jove, Dermot Windleband, one of the master-brains of our time, could see the stuff in him.

'It's very kind of you to say so, Mr Windleband,' he murmured, diffidently.

'Bosh! Shouldn't say it if I didn't mean it,' was the brusque rejoinder. 'I *have* taken a fancy to you – so much so, that I'm going to do for you what I very seldom do for any man.'

Roland said something futile about too much having been done for him already. Dermot waved the suggestion aside.

'Nonsense – only too glad. Now look here, Bleke; as a general rule I don't give tips—'

'You're quite right,' agreed Roland, warmly. 'I think the tipping system is iniquitous. It ought to be abolished.'

'Ah – I don't mean that sort of tip,' said Dermot, with an indulgent smile; 'I mean a financial tip. I suppose you don't know much about investments?'

'Not a thing,' confessed Roland. Candour would, he felt, be best in the circumstances. No use attempting to bluff with Master-Minds.

'Put your money,' said Dermot, sinking his voice to a cautious whisper, as though he feared that the very walls might hear and make public the priceless secret, 'put every penny you can afford into Wildcat Reefs.'

He leaned back in his chair with the benign air of, say, the Philosopher who has just imparted to a favourite disciple the recently-discovered secret of the Elixir of Life. A pregnant silence hung for a few moments over the room.

'Thank you very much, Mr Windleband,' said Roland, when the overmastering sense of gratitude with which he was filled would allow him to speak. 'I will.'

Once more were the Napoleonic features lightened by that rare, indulgent smile.

'Not so fast, young man,' he laughed. 'Getting into Wildcat Reefs isn't quite so easy as you seem to think. Now – how much did you propose to invest?'

'About thirty thousand pounds.'

Roland tried to mention the sum in a casual, off-hand way, as though it were a mere nothing; but the effort was not a success. A note of pride would insist upon creeping into his voice.

'Thirty thousand pounds!' exclaimed Dermot. 'Why, my dear

fellow, if it got about that you were going to buy Wildcat Reefs on that scale the market would be convulsed.'

Which was true enough. If it had got about on 'Change that anyone was going to invest thirty thousand pounds in Wildcat Reefs the market would certainly have been convulsed. The House would have rocked with laughter. Wildcat Reefs were a standing joke – except with the unfortunate few who still held any of the shares.

'The thing will have to be done very cautiously,' Dermot went on. 'No one must know. But I think – only *think*, mind you – that I can manage it for you.'

'You're awfully kind, Mr Windleband,' murmured Roland, gratefully.

'Not at all, my dear boy, not at all. As a matter of fact, I shall be doing another pal of mine a good turn at the same time.'

'Another pal!' Gratifying words, these, from a Master-Mind. Roland felt that he was coming into his own apace. Few young fellows of his age, he was pretty certain, could count Windlebands amongst their friends.

'This pal of mine,' Dermot proceeded, 'has a large holding of Wildcats. He wants to realize in order to put the money into something else, in which he is more personally interested. But, of course, he couldn't unload thirty thousand pounds' worth of Wildcats on the public market.'

'No, no – I quite see that,' assented Roland. Dermot glanced up at him quickly, wondering whether, after all, he knew a little more than he had appeared to do. Luckily, Roland was trying, at the moment, to look intelligent, so Dermot was reassured.

'It might, however, be done by private negotiation. I daresay I could manage it for you; and probably I could do the deal on very favourable terms. Very possibly – as he wants the money in a hurry – he might let you have the shares at as low, say, as one and a half. I'm not sure, mind you; but it might be done.'

'What do Wildcats stand at now?' inquired Roland, timidly. Dermot smiled at him, pityingly.

'They're never quoted,' he replied. 'There's no market in them, you see. In the ordinary way nobody ever sells Wildcats. I don't suppose a hundred pounds' worth have changed hands in the last six months.'

All of which, again, was perfectly true.

Then Dermot read Roland an article on Wildcats in *The City Eagle* – a financial organ with which Roland was unacquainted. As Dermot had had to pay one hundred pounds for the article in question he was to be excused for the enthusiasm with which he spoke of the writer's gifts and of the high opinion in which he held his judgement. From what was said in the article Roland rather gathered that, compared with Wildcat Reefs, the Bank of England was a risky concern in which to put one's money.

Two days later Roland Bleke became the proud possessor of twenty thousand one-pound shares in the Wildcat Reel Goldmine, and Dermot Windleband gave his bank a glad surprise by paying in thirty thousand pounds to his account.

It was not, perhaps, till four days later that Dermot again came back from the City with the worried look. Mrs Windleband could not understand it. Never – even in the most desperate crises – had she known the Napoleon of Finance to look in the least perturbed. She wondered what could be the cause.

When Dermot told her – which he did while they were dressing – her eyes grew big with horror. She could not believe it.

'Good heavens!' she exclaimed. 'You can't mean it! Dermot – I've known you to do silly, almost inexcusable things in your time; but this – this – is positively criminal!'

Her husband winced at the words, but he did not attempt to deny the justice of her accusation.

'If he sees the papers in the morning—!'

'He mustn't! He shan't!'

She walked restlessly up and down the room, trying to think of a plan.

'We must try and keep it from him – for tomorrow, at least,' she said, at last. 'Go up to town by the early train – he won't be down – and take all the papers with you. While you're away I'll try to think out something.'

'You're a dear, sweet soul.'

He made as though to embrace her; but she pushed his arm away, almost roughly.

'Don't!' she cried. 'I couldn't bear to kiss you, when I think of what you've done.'

Dermot bowed his head meekly before the storm of her indignation.

'I – I'm awfully sorry, Lal,' he stammered, brokenly. 'I had no idea—'

'Stop! Stop!' she interrupted. 'Be quiet. Let me think how on earth I'm to get you out of this ghastly mess you've landed us in.'

'Mr Bleke – don't go. I want to speak to you.'

Roland stared in astonishment at his hostess. Never before had he seen Mrs Windleband exhibit the slightest sign of anything that could be construed as agitation. She had always struck him as the calmest woman he had ever met. Nothing ever ruffled her. But now she looked pale and anxious. There were great dark rings under her eyes, which were red, as if she had been crying.

'Please shut the door – and make sure that none of the servants are about.'

Roland obeyed her, wondering what in the world it all meant.

'Mr Bleke,' she began, in faltering accents, when he had come back to the tea-table, 'promise me – on your word of honour – that you will never speak to a living soul of what I am going to tell you.'

Roland gave her to understand that, compared with him, the tomb would be a chatterbox.

'Mr Bleke – I don't know how to tell you – but my husband has swindled you!'

The poor woman's distress, as she made the hateful confession, was pathetic to witness. Agitated and shocked as Roland was by the disturbing intelligence which she had just imparted, his heart was filled with pity for her.

'Swindled me? Your husband swindled me, Mrs Windleband! I can't believe it.'

'Neither could I, at first – when he confessed it to me,' came the reply, in heart-broken accents. 'But it's only too dreadfully true. He told me last night, and, Mr Bleke, I haven't known a minute's peace since. I cried all night; and this morning I made up my mind that I must let you know everything and – and try to make what reparation I can!'

Mrs Windleband's further utterance was choked by a storm of sobs. Whilst he had every sympathy with her distress, Roland wished Mrs Windleband would not take her husband's delinquencies quite so much to heart. Without any desire to hurry her unduly over her lamentations, Roland felt a pardonable anxiety to know how – but perhaps more particularly of how much – he had been swindled by her villainous husband.

Presently Mrs Windleband recovered sufficiently to explain:

'It was over those shares he sold to you – those Wildc-c-cats! They're worthless!' And then there came a fresh deluge.

Wildcats worthless! Roland's heart stopped beating.

'Oh, Mr Bleke, forgive him, please!' pleaded Mrs Windleband, holding out her clasped hands in a gesture of entreaty. 'You don't know how he was tempted. People were pressing him for money on every side – he has so many enemies – he didn't know where to turn – ruin was staring him in the face! And then, when you came along with all that money at your disposal – it was t-t-too much for him!'

'Can't quite see that,' was Roland's rueful reply. 'If it was too much for him, why couldn't he have left me some of it, instead of taking pretty well every shilling I've got!'

'How much did you pay for the shares?' asked Mrs Windleband, ignoring Roland's last remark.

'Thirty thousand pounds – that's what he had out of me for them,' said Roland, bitterly.

'Oh, thank Heaven, thank Heaven!' cried Mrs Windleband, in accents of heartfelt relief. For his part, Roland could see nothing whatever to thank Heaven for; and he said so.

'Ah, but if it's no more than thirty thousand pounds I can put everything right again,' explained Mrs Windleband, joyfully. 'Or very nearly, at all events.'

Thirty thousand pounds, it occurred to Roland, was a little matter which would take some putting right. He felt some curiosity as to how Mrs Windleband proposed to do it.

'Why, I have some money of my own, you see,' she explained. 'I wouldn't let Dermot have it, though he begged me ever so hard, because I wanted to have something secured for us to live on, in case the worst came to the worst. But I would rather part with my last penny and die in the gutter than have Dermot dishonoured!'

With trembling fingers she drew out of her bag a cheque-book.

Then she sat down at the writing-table and proceeded to make out a cheque.

'I shall have to post-date it about a month,' she said, apologetically, to Roland, 'to give me time, you know, to realize the securities in which my money is invested. Do you mind?'

'But, really, Mrs Windleband, I can't allow this,' protested Roland. 'It is too generous of you. You must not beggar yourself for your husband's sake. After all, I bought the shares with my eyes open—'

'If you don't let me buy them back from you I shall go mad and probably kill myself,' declared Mrs Windleband, hysterically. 'I should never know another minute's happiness as long as I lived, if I did not right the wrong which my husband has done to you.'

She signed the cheque and, tearing it out of the book, handed it over to Roland.

'If you will just give me some sort of receipt, saying that this is for shares which you will have transferred to me as soon as the necessary documents can be signed, that will make an end of the whole dreadful business, and my mind will be at rest again,' she said.

For just one second Roland hesitated – but only for one second. Then he handed the cheque back.

'I can't take your money, Mrs Windleband, really I can't,' he said, simply. 'It's noble and generous in the extreme of you to offer to make this sacrifice, but I can't accept it. I've still got a little money left; and I've always been used to working for my living, anyhow. I – I – can't tell you how I admire you – but tear this up, please.'

'Mr Bleke – I implore you!' She had flung herself on her knees before him and was making frenzied efforts to thrust the cheque back into his hands.

This was the moment selected by Parkinson, the impeccable butler of the Windleband establishment, to enter the room. The scene which met his eyes may have surprised Parkinson, but no trace of this betrayed itself upon his calm, immobile features. In his hand he had an evening paper, which he gave to Roland.

'The paper which you asked me to get for you, sir.'

That was all he said. And then he withdrew.

'Parkinson told me he was going down to the village this afternoon, so I asked him to get me an evening paper,' explained Roland, apologetically. 'I wanted to see how the Test Match was going.'

He was just about to throw the paper carelessly aside – for who, at a moment of such dramatic stress as that through which he was just passing, wanted to read about Test Matches? – when a flaring headline which ran right across the front page arrested his eye.

'Why!' he exclaimed. 'It says something here about Wildcats!'

'Does it?' Mrs Windleband's voice sounded strangely dull and toneless. Her eyes were closed and she was swaying to and fro, as if she were just about to faint.

Roland had not over-stated the case. There certainly was something about Wildcats. Indeed, there was hardly anything about anything except Wildcats. Even the Test Match was relegated to the back page.

This was what the headlines alone had to say:

THE WILDCAT REEF GOLD-MINE
ANOTHER KLONDYKE
FRENZIED SCENES ON THE STOCK EXCHANGE
BROKERS FIGHT FOR SHARES
RECORD BOOM
UNPRECEDENTED RISE IN PRICES

Shorn of all superfluous adjectives and general journalistic exuberance, what the paper had to announce to its readers was this:

The 'special commissioner' sent out by the *Financial Argus* to make an exhaustive examination of the Wildcat Reef Mine – with the amiable view, no doubt, of exploding Dermot Windleband once and for all with the confiding British public – had found, to his unbounded astonishment, that there were vast quantities of gold in the mine.

The publication of their expert's report in the *Financial Argus* had resulted in a boom in Wildcat Reefs the like of which had never before been known on the Stock Exchange. In less than two days the one-pound shares had gone up from something like one shilling and sixpence per bundle to nearly ten pounds a share, and even at this latter figure people were literally fighting to secure them.

As she read the pregnant news over Roland's shoulder, Mrs Windleband burst once more into expressions of gratitude to Providence.

'Oh, thank Heaven, thank Heaven!' she cried, hysterically. 'Then my Dermot was not swindling you after all! He must have known all the time that the shares were going to rise like this. He said something about it when he told me that he had sold the shares to you, but I didn't believe him. I thought it was only an excuse. Oh – how I have misjudged my poor dear darling!' She dabbed pathetically at her weeping eyes. 'I feel so happy, so relieved, that I must go to my room and have a real good cry!'

Roland made no effort to deter her. He was too dazed to do anything. So far as his reeling brain was capable of mathematical calculation he figured that he was now worth about two hundred thousand pounds. It was an awesome thought.

Down the corridor Mrs Windleband ran into her husband – just returned from the City. He looked at her, inquiringly. She shook her head.

'No go!' was all she said.

But Dermot said a great deal more than that.

It was one of those hard, nubbly rolls. The best restaurants charge you sixpence for having the good sense not to eat them. It hit Roland Bleke with considerable vehemence on the bridge of the nose. For the moment Roland fancied that the roof of the Regent Grill-room must have fallen in; and, as this would automatically put an end to the party, he was not altogether sorry. He had never been to a theatrical supper-party before, and within five minutes of his arrival at the present one he had become afflicted with an intense desire never to go to a theatrical supper-party again. To be a success at these gay gatherings one must possess dash; and Roland, whatever his other sterling qualities, was a little short of dash.

The young man on the other side of the table was quite nice about it. While not actually apologizing, he went so far as to explain that it was 'old Gerry' whom he had had in his mind when he started the roll on its course. After a glance at 'old Gerry' – a chinless child of about nineteen – Roland felt that it would be churlish to be angry with a young man whose intentions had been so wholly admirable. 'Old Gerry' had one of those faces in which any alteration, even the comparatively limited one which a roll would be capable of producing, was bound to be for the better. He smiled a sickly smile and said that it didn't matter.

The charming creature who sat on his assailant's left, however, took a more serious view of the situation.

'Sidney, you make me tired,' she said, severely. 'If I had thought you didn't know how to act like a gentleman I wouldn't have come here with you. Go away somewhere and throw bread at yourself; and ask Mr Bleke to come and sit by me. I want to talk to him.'

That was Roland's first introduction to Miss Billy Verepoint.

'I've been wanting to have a chat with you all the evening, Mr Bleke,' she said, as Roland blushingly sank into the empty chair. 'I've heard such a lot about you.'

What Miss Verepoint had heard about Roland was that he had two hundred thousand pounds and apparently did not know what to do with it.

'In fact, if I hadn't been told that you would be here, I shouldn't have come to this party. Can't stand these gatherings of Nuts in May as a general rule. They bore me stiff.'

Roland hastily revised his first estimate of the theatrical profession. Shallow, empty-headed creatures some of them might be, no doubt, but there were exceptions. Here was a girl of real discernment – a thoughtful student of character – a girl who understood that a man might sit at a supper-party without uttering a word and might still be a man of parts.

'I'm afraid you'll think me very outspoken – but that's me all over. All my friends say, "Billy Verepoint's a funny girl: if she likes anyone she just tells them so straight out; and if she doesn't like anyone she tells them straight out, too."'

'And a very admirable trait,' said Roland, enthusiastically.

Miss Verepoint sighed. 'P'r'aps it is,' she said, pensively; 'but I'm afraid it's what has kept me back in my profession. Managers don't like it; they think girls should be seen and not heard.'

Roland's blood boiled. Managers were plainly a dastardly crew.

'But what's the good of worrying,' went on Miss Verepoint, with a brave but hollow laugh. 'Of course, it's wearing, having to wait when one has got as much ambition as I have; but they all tell me that my chance is bound to come some day.'

The intense mournfulness of Miss Verepoint's expression seemed to indicate that she anticipated the arrival of the desired day not less than sixty years hence. Roland was profoundly moved. His chivalrous nature was up in arms. He fell to wondering if he could do anything to help this victim of managerial unfairness.

'You don't mind my going on about my troubles, do you?' asked Miss Verepoint, solicitously. 'One so seldom meets anybody really sympathetic.'

Roland babbled fervent assurances, and she pressed his hand gratefully.

'I wonder if you would care to come to tea one afternoon?' she said.

'Oh, rather!' said Roland. He would have liked to put it in a more polished way, but he was almost beyond speech.

'Of course, I know what a busy man you are—'

'No, no!'

'Well, I should be in tomorrow afternoon, if you cared to look in.'

Roland bleated gratefully.

'I'll write down the address for you,' said Miss Verepoint, suddenly business-like.

Exactly when he committed himself to the purchase of the Windsor Theatre, Roland could never say. The idea seemed to come into existence fully grown, without preliminary discussion.

One moment it was not – the next it was. His recollections of the afternoon which he spent drinking luke-warm tea and punctuating Miss Verepoint's flow of speech with yeses and noes were always so thoroughly confused that he never knew even whose suggestion it was. All he knew was that he left the flat the accredited champion of its owner, the Perseus who was to rescue this theatrical Andromeda from the rock of obscurity to which a series of monsters in the shape of managers had chained her. It was bewildering and, when he allowed his mind to dwell on the probable cost of the rescue, not unmixedly pleasant. But for the moment the romantic side of his character was so much in the ascendant that his native prudence was almost completely stifled. His exuberant fancy was playing lightly round the rosy vision of himself bearing away this divine creature from the competing bachelor peers of England, and the fact that in a single afternoon he had committed himself to an outlay of an indefinite number of thousands of pounds had not yet had time to take its proper place as a factor in the situation.

The purchase of a West-end theatre, when one has the necessary cash, is not nearly such a complicated business as the layman might imagine. Roland was staggered by the rapidity with which the transaction was carried through. The theatre was his before he had time to realize that he had never meant to buy the thing at all. He had gone into the offices of Mr Montague with the intention of making an offer for the lease for, say, six months; and that wizard, in the space of less than an hour, had not only induced him to sign mysterious documents which made him sole proprietor of the house, but had left him with the feeling that he had done an extremely acute stroke of business. Mr Montague had dabbled in many professions in his time, from street peddling upwards, but what he was really best at was hypnotism.

Although he felt, after the spell of Mr Montague's magnetism was withdrawn, rather like a nervous man who has been given a large baby to hold by a strange woman who has promptly vanished round the corner, Roland was to some extent consoled by the praise bestowed upon him by Miss Verepoint. She said it was much better to buy a theatre than to rent it, because then you escaped the heavy rent. It was specious, but Roland had a dim feeling that there was a flaw somewhere in the reasoning; and it was from this point that a shadow may be said to have fallen upon the brightness of the venture.

He would have been even less self-congratulatory if he had known the Windsor Theatre's reputation. Being a comparative stranger in the Metropolis, he was unaware that its nickname in theatrical circles was 'The Mugs' Graveyard' – a title which had been bestowed upon it not without reason. Built originally by a slightly insane old gentleman, whose principal delusion was that the public was pining for a constant supply of the higher drama, and more especially those specimens of the higher drama which flowed practically without cessation from the restless pen of the insane old gentleman himself, the Windsor Theatre had passed from hand to hand with the agility of a gold watch in a gathering of racecourse thieves. The one anxiety of the unhappy man who found himself, by some accident, in possession of the Windsor Theatre, was to pass it on to somebody else. The only really permanent tenant it ever had was the representative of the Official Receiver. The record run achieved there was one of ten nights, and four of these would never have happened if the company had discovered at an earlier date that the gentleman who was supposed to be responsible for their salaries had left by the Wednesday boat for America.

Various causes were assigned for the phenomenal ill-luck of

the theatre, but undoubtedly the vital objection to it as a Temple of Drama lay in the fact that nobody could ever find the place where it was hidden. Cabmen shook their heads on the rare occasions when they were asked to take a fare there. Explorers to whom a stroll through the Australian bush was child's play had been known to spend an hour on its trail and finish up at the point where they had started.

It was precisely this quality of elusiveness which had first attracted Mr Montague. He was a far-seeing man, and to him the topographical advantages of the theatre were enormous. It was farther from a fire-station than any other building of the same insurance value in London, even without having regard to the mystery which enveloped its whereabouts. Often after a good dinner he would lean comfortably back in his chair and see in the smoke of his cigar a vision of the Windsor Theatre blazing merrily, while distracted firemen galloped madly all over London, vainly endeavouring to get someone to direct them to the scene of the conflagration. So Mr Montague bought the theatre for a mere song, and prepared to get busy. Unluckily for him, the representatives of the various fire-offices with which he had effected his policies got busy first. The generous fellows insisted upon taking off his shoulders the burden of maintaining the fireman whose permanent presence in a theatre is required by law. Nothing would satisfy them but to install firemen of their own and pay their salaries. This, to a man in whom the instincts of the phoenix were so strongly developed as they were in Mr Montague, was distinctly disconcerting. He saw himself making no profit on the deal – a thing which had never happened to him before. And then Roland Bleke occurred, and Mr Montague's belief that his race was really chosen was restored. He sold the Windsor Theatre to Roland for twenty-five thousand pounds.

It was fifteen thousand pounds more than he himself had given for it, and this very satisfactory profit mitigated the slight regret which he felt when it came to transferring to Roland the insurance policies. To have effected policies amounting to rather more than seventy thousand pounds on a building so notoriously valueless as the Windsor Theatre had been an achievement of which Mr Montague was justly proud; and it seemed sad to him that so much earnest endeavour should be thrown away.

Over the little lunch with which she kindly allowed Roland to entertain her, to celebrate the purchase of the theatre, Miss Verepoint outlined her policy.

'What we must put up at that theatre,' she announced, 'is a revue.'

What they would be far better advised to put up, Roland felt, was a board with 'To be Let' painted on it in the largest possible lettering.

'A revue,' went on Miss Verepoint, making as she spoke little calculations on the back of the menu, 'we could run for about fifteen hundred a week – or, say, two thousand.'

Saying two thousand, thought Roland to himself, is not quite the same as paying two thousand, so why should she stint herself?

'I know two boys who could write us a topping revue,' said Miss Verepoint. 'They'd spread themselves, too, if it was for me. They're in love with me – both of them. We'd better get in touch with them at once.'

To Roland there seemed to be something just the least bit sinister about the sound of that word 'touch,' but he said nothing.

'Why, there they are – lunching over there!' cried Miss Verepoint, pointing to a neighbouring table. 'Now, isn't that lucky?'

To Roland the luck was not quite so apparent, but he made no demur to Miss Verepoint's suggestion that they should be brought over to their table.

The two boys as to whose capabilities to write a topping revue Miss Verepoint had formed so optimistic an estimate proved to be well-grown lads of about forty-five and forty respectively. Of the two, Roland thought that perhaps R. P. de Parys was a shade the more obnoxious, but a closer inspection left him with the feeling that these fine distinctions were a little unfair with men of such equal talents. Bromham Rhodes ran his friend so close that it was practically a dead-heat. They were both very fat and somewhat bulgy-eyed. This was due to the fact that what revue-writing exacts from its exponents is the constant assimilation of food and drink. Bromham Rhodes had the largest appetite in London; but, on the other hand, R. P. de Parys was a better drinker.

'Well, dear old thing!' said Bromham Rhodes.

'Well, old child!' said R. P. de Parys.

Both these remarks were addressed to Miss Verepoint. The talented pair appeared to be unaware of Roland's existence.

Miss Verepoint struck the business note.

'Now you stop, boys,' she said. 'Tie weights to yourselves and sink down into those chairs. I want you two lads to write a revue for me.'

'Delighted!' said Bromham Rhodes. 'But—'

'There is the trifling point to be raised first—' said R. P. de Parys.

'Where is the money coming from?' said Bromham Rhodes.

'My friend, Mr Bleke, is putting up the money,' said Miss Verepoint, with dignity. 'He has taken the Windsor Theatre.'

The interest of the two authors in their host, till then languid, increased with a jerk. They unbent quite a lot.

'Has he? By Jove!' they cried. 'We must get together and talk this over.'

It was Roland's first experience of a theatrical talking-over, and he never forgot it. Two such talkers-over as Bromham Rhodes and R. P. de Parys were scarcely to be found in the length and breadth of theatrical London. Nothing, it seemed, could the gifted pair even begin to think of doing without first discussing the proposition in all its aspects. The amount of food which Roland found himself compelled to absorb during the course of these debates was appalling. Discussions which began at lunch would be continued until it was time to order dinner; and then, as likely as not, they would have to sit there till supper-time in order to thrash the question thoroughly out.

The collection of a cast was a matter even more complicated than the actual composition of the revue. There was the almost insuperable difficulty that Miss Verepoint firmly vetoed every name suggested. It seemed practically impossible to find any man or woman in all England or America whose peculiar gifts or lack of them would not interfere with Miss Verepoint's giving a satisfactory performance of the principal *rôle*. It was all very perplexing to Roland; but as Miss Verepoint was an expert in theatrical matters, he scarcely felt entitled to question her views.

It was about this time that Roland proposed to Miss Verepoint. The passage of time and the strain of talking over the revue had to a certain extent moderated his original fervour. He had shaded off from a passionate devotion, through various diminishing tints of regard for her, into a sort of pale sunset glow of affection. His principal reason for proposing was that it seemed to him to be in the natural order of events. Her air towards him had become distinctly proprietorial. She now called him 'Roly-Poly' in public, a proceeding which left him with mixed feelings. Also, she had taken to ordering him about, which, as everybody knows, is an unmistakable sign of affection among ladies of the theatrical profession. Finally, in his chivalrous way, Roland had begun to feel a little apprehensive lest he might be compromising Miss Verepoint. Everybody knew that he was putting up the money for the revue in which she was to appear. They were constantly seen together at restaurants. People looked arch when they spoke to him about her. He had to ask himself: Was he behaving like a perfect gentleman? The answer was in the negative. He took a cab to her flat and proposed before he could repent of his decision.

She accepted him. He was not certain for a moment whether he was glad or sorry.

'But I don't want to get married,' she went on, 'until I have justified my choice of a profession. You will have to wait until I have made a success in this revue.'

Roland was shocked to find himself hugely relieved at this concession.

The revue took shape. There did apparently exist a handful of artistes to whom Miss Verepoint had no objection, and these – a scrubby but confident lot – were promptly engaged. Sallow Americans sprang from nowhere with songs, dances, and ideas for effects. Tousled-haired scenic artists wandered in with model scenes under their arms. A great crowd of chorus ladies settled upon the theatre like flies. Even Bromham Rhodes and R. P. de Parys – those human pythons – showed signs of activity. They cornered Roland one day near Swan and Edgar's, steered him into the Piccadilly grill-room, and over a hearty lunch read him extracts from a brown paper-covered manuscript which, they informed him, was the first act.

It looked a battered sort of manuscript, and, indeed, it had every right to be. Under various titles and at various times, Bromham Rhodes's and R. P. de Parys's first act had been refused by practically every responsible manager in London. As 'Oh! What a Life!' it had failed to satisfy the directors of the Empire. Rechristened 'Wow-Wow,' it had been rejected by the Alhambra. The Hippodrome had refused to consider it, even under the name of 'Hullo, Cellar-Flap!' It was now called 'Pass Along, Please!' and, according to its authors, was a real revue.

Roland was to learn, as the days went on, that in the world in which he was moving everything was Real Revue that was not a Stunt or a Corking Effect. He floundered in the sea of Real Revue, Stunts, and Corking Effects. As far as he could gather, the main difference between these things was that real revue was something which had been stolen from some previous English production, whereas a stunt or a corking effect was something which had been looted from New York. A judicious blend of these, he was given to understand, constituted the sort of thing the public wanted.

Rehearsals began before, in Roland's opinion, his little army was properly supplied with ammunition. True, they had the first act, but even the authors agreed that it wanted bringing up-to-date in parts. They explained that it was, in a manner of speaking, their life-work: that they had actually started it about ten years ago when they were careless lads. Inevitably, it was spotted here and there with smart topical hits of the early years of the century; but that, they said, would be all right. They could freshen it up in a couple of evenings; it was simply a matter of deleting allusions to pro-Boers and substituting lines about Marconi shares and mangel-wurzels.

'It'll be all right,' they assured Roland; 'this is Real Revue.'

It was not only the ammunition that was lacking; the army itself was far from being at full strength. Unless each of the present corps of artistes played several parts simultaneously, he could not see how the work was to be staged at all. Pitying experts corrected his views on this point. This, they explained, was precisely where the stunts and corking effects were to come in.

'Right here,' said the American producer, 'I bring on the gurls. During this scene they've been arkupying the back row of the orchestra chairs, dressed as young fellers about town – same what you call nuts. At the cue they come up the joy-way in a bunch, flashing searchlights at the audience and singing, "You were here with another gurl last night." It's a corking effect. They did it in N'York last fall. That gives your comedian time to get off and change and come on again as Mrs Pankhurst.'

In times of trouble there is always a point at which one may say, 'Here is the beginning of the end.' This point came with Roland with the commencement of the rehearsals. Till then he had not fully realized the terrible nature of the production for which he had made himself responsible. Moreover, it was rehearsals which gave him his first clear insight into the depths of the character of Miss Verepoint.

Miss Verepoint was not at her best at rehearsals. For the first time, as he watched her, Roland found himself feeling that there was a case to be made out for the managers who had so consistently kept her in the background. Miss Verepoint, to use the technical term, threw her weight about. There were not many good lines in the script of Act I of 'Pass Along, Please!' but such as there were she reached out for and grabbed away from their owners, who retired into corners, scowling and muttering, like dogs robbed of bones. She snubbed everybody, Roland included. The only gleam of brightness about her performance was that she must have reduced the weight of Bromham Rhodes and R. P. de Parys at the rate of quite a pound a day.

Roland sat in the cold darkness of the stalls and watched her, panic-stricken. Like an icy wave, it had swept over him what marriage with this girl would mean. He suddenly realized how essentially domestic his instincts really were. Life with Miss Verepoint would mean perpetual dinners at restaurants, bread-throwing suppers, motor-rides – everything that he hated most. Yet, as a man of honour, he was tied to her. If the revue was a success, she would marry him; and revues, he knew, were always successes. At that very moment there were six 'best revues in London' running at various theatres. He shuddered at the thought that in a few weeks there would be seven.

He felt a longing for rural solitude. He wanted to be alone by himself for a day or two in a place where there were no papers with advertisements of revues, no grill-rooms, and, above all, no Miss Billy Verepoint. That night he stole away to a Norfolk village, where, in happier days, he had once spent a summer holi-day – a peaceful, primitive place where the inhabitants believed in witchcraft, disbelieved in drainage systems, and could not have told real revue from a corking effect.

Here, for the space of a week, Roland lay in hiding, while his quivering nerves gradually recovered tone. He returned to London happier, but a little apprehensive. Beyond a brief tele-gram of farewell, he had not communicated with Miss Verepoint for seven days, and experience had made him aware that she was a lady who demanded an adequate amount of attention.

That his nervous system was not wholly restored to health was borne in upon him as he walked along Piccadilly on his way to his flat; for, when somebody suddenly slapped him hard between the shoulder-blades, he uttered a stifled yell and leaped into the air.

Turning to face his assailant, he found himself meeting the genial gaze of Mr Montague, his predecessor in the ownership of the Windsor Theatre.

Mr Montague was effusively friendly, and, for some mysterious reason, congratulatory.

'You've done it, have you? You pulled it off, did you? And in the first month – by George! And I took you for the plain, ordinary mug of commerce! My boy, you're as deep as they make 'em. Who'd have thought it to look at you? It was the greatest idea anyone ever had – and staring me in the face all the time and I never saw it! But I don't grudge it to you – you deserve it, my boy! You're a nut!'

'I really don't know what you mean.'

'Quite right, my boy!' chuckled Mr Montague. 'You're quite right to keep it up, even among friends. It don't do to risk anything, and the least said soonest mended.'

He went on his way, leaving Roland completely mystified.

Voices from his sitting-room, among which he recognized the high note of Miss Verepoint, reminded him of the ordeal before him. He entered with what he hoped was a careless ease of manner, but his heart was beating fast. Since the opening of rehearsals he had acquired a wholesome respect for Miss Verepoint's tongue. She was sitting in his favourite chair. There were also present Bromham Rhodes and R. P. de Parys, who had made themselves completely at home with a couple of his cigars and whiskey from the oldest bin.

'So here you are at last!' said Miss Verepoint, querulously. 'The valet told us you were expected back this morning, so we waited.

Where on earth have you been to, running away like this, without a word?'

'I only went—'

'Well, it doesn't matter where you went. The main point is, what are you going to do about it?'

'We thought we'd better come along and talk it over,' said R. P. de Parys.

'It's curry day at the Savoy,' put in Bromham Rhodes helpfully.

'Talk what over?' said Roland. 'The revue?'

'Oh, don't try and be funny, for goodness' sake!' snapped Miss Verepoint. 'It doesn't suit you. You haven't the right shape of head. What do you suppose we want to talk over? The theatre, of course.'

'What about the theatre?'

Miss Verepoint looked searchingly at him. 'You don't mean to say you really haven't heard! Don't you ever read the papers?'

'I haven't seen a paper since I went away.'

There was an impressive silence. The three looked at one another.

'Well, better have it quick and not waste time breaking it gently,' said Miss Verepoint. 'The theatre's been burnt down – that's what's happened!'

'Burnt down?'

'Drink this!' said Bromham Rhodes, hospitably, extending his glass.

'Bear up,' said R. P. de Parys, relighting his cigar.

'Burnt down!' repeated Roland.

'That's what I said, didn't I? The Suffragettes did it. They left copies of *Votes for Women* about the place. The silly asses set fire to two other theatres as well, but they happened to be in main thoroughfares, and the fire-brigade got them under at once.

I suppose they couldn't find the Windsor. Anyhow, it's burnt to the ground and what we want to know is what are you going to do about it?'

Roland was much too busy blessing the good angels of Kingsway to reply at once. R. P. de Parys, sympathetic soul, placed a wrong construction on his silence.

'Poor old Roly!' he said. 'It's quite broken him up. The best thing we can do is all to go off and talk it over at the Savoy over a bit of lunch.'

'It's curry day,' said Bromham Rhodes.

'No,' said Miss Verepoint. 'We can talk it over much more quietly here.'

R. P. de Parys and Bromham Rhodes groaned hungrily. It was certainly true that they could talk it over more quietly without the accompaniment of neighbouring Germans crooning over their soup, but it was not their idea of a talking-over at all.

'Well,' said Miss Verepoint, 'what are you going to do – rebuild the Windsor or try and get another theatre?'

The authors were all for rebuilding the Windsor. True, it would take time, but it would be more satisfactory in every way. Besides, at this time of the year it would be no easy matter to secure another theatre at a moment's notice.

To R. P. de Parys and Bromham Rhodes the destruction of the Windsor Theatre had appeared less in the light of a disaster than as a direct intervention on the part of Providence. The completion of that tiresome second act, which had brooded over their lives like an ugly cloud, could now be postponed indefinitely.

'Of course,' said R. P. de Parys, thoughtfully, 'our contract with you makes it obligatory on you to produce our revue by a certain date; but I dare say, Bromham, we could meet Roly there, couldn't we?'

'Sure!' said Rhodes. 'Something nominal – say a further five hundred on account of fees – would satisfy us. I certainly think it would be better to rebuild the Windsor, don't you, R. P.?'

'I do,' agreed R. P. de Parys, cordially. 'You see, Roly, our revue has been written to fit the Windsor. It would be very difficult to alter it for production at another theatre. Yes, I feel sure that rebuilding the Windsor would be your best course.'

There was a pause.

'What do you think, Roly-Poly?' asked Miss Verepoint, as Roland made no sign. Roland, though, had been putting in some very earnest thinking, and now his mind was made up.

'Nothing would delight me more than to rebuild the Windsor, or to take another theatre, or do anything else to oblige,' he said, cheerfully. 'Unfortunately, I have no more money to burn.'

It was as if a bomb had suddenly exploded in the room. A dreadful silence fell upon his hearers. For the moment no one spoke. R. P. de Parys woke with a start out of a beautiful dream of prawn curry and Bromham Rhodes forgot that he had not tasted food for nearly two hours. Miss Verepoint was the first to break the silence.

'Do you mean to say,' she gasped, 'that you didn't insure the place?'

Roland shook his head. The particular form in which Miss Verepoint had put the question entitled him, he felt, to make this answer.

'Why didn't you?' Miss Verepoint's tone was almost menacing.

'Because it did not appear to me to be necessary.'

Nor was it necessary, said Roland to his conscience; Mr Montague had done all the insuring that was necessary – and a bit over.

Miss Verepoint fought with her growing indignation, and lost.

'What about the salaries of the people who have been rehearsing all this time?' she demanded.

'I'm sorry that they should be out of an engagement, but it is scarcely my fault. However, I propose to give each of them a month's salary. I can manage that, I think.'

Miss Verepoint rose. 'And what about me? What about me? That's what I want to know. Where do *I* get off? If you think I'm going to marry you without your getting a theatre and putting up this revue you're jolly well mistaken.'

Roland made a gesture which was intended to convey regret and resignation. He even contrived to sigh.

'Very well, then,' said Miss Verepoint, rightly interpreting this behaviour as his final pronouncement on the situation. 'Then everything's jolly well off.'

She swept out of the room, the two authors following in her wake like porpoises behind a liner. Roland went to his bureau, unlocked it, and took out a bundle of documents. He let his fingers stray lovingly among the fire insurance policies which energetic Mr Montague had been at such pains to secure from so many companies.

'And so,' he said softly to himself, 'am I.'

It was with a start that Roland Bleke realized that the girl at the other end of the bench was crying. For the last few minutes, as far as his preoccupation allowed him to notice them at all, he had been attributing the subdued sniffs to a summer cold.

He was embarrassed. He blamed the fate that had led him to this particular bench, and also the economy which had caused him to select a bench instead of taking a pennyworth of green chair – an economy all the more ridiculous because his reason for sitting down at all was that he wished to give himself up to quiet deliberation on the question of what on earth he was to do with two hundred and fifty thousand pounds, to which figure his fortune had now risen.

It was an intermittent source of annoyance to him that he could not succeed entirely in shaking off his old prudent self. Here he was with wealth beyond the dreams of avarice – at any rate, of his own avarice – and yet he still kept catching himself in the act of approaching the world from the point of view of a provincial seed-merchant's second clerk. He longed to live with a gay spaciousness, but habit was occasionally too strong for him. Sometimes he would ask himself despairingly if the rules of the new life were not too hard to learn; and for some days after one of these black moments he was apt to behave like a largesse-distributing monarch gone mad. Waiters, porters, cab-men, and others who came within reach of him at such times would dream of retiring with fortunes.

The sniffs continued. Roland's discomfort increased. Chivalry had always been his weakness. In the old days, on a hundred and forty pounds a year, he had had few opportunities of indulging himself in this direction; but now it seemed to him sometimes that the whole world was crying out for assistance. When the world gets within earshot of a chivalrous young man with plenty of spare cash, it is not apt to be reticent.

Should he speak to her? He wanted to; but only a few days ago his eye had been caught by the placard of a weekly paper bearing the title of *Squibs*, on which in large letters was the legend, 'Men Who Speak to Girls,' and he had gathered that the accompanying article was a denunciation rather than a eulogy of these individuals. On the other hand, she was obviously in distress.

Another sniff decided him.

'I say, you know,' he said.

What he had meant to say was, 'Pardon me, but you appear to be in trouble. Is there anything I can do for you?' But the difference between life and the stage is that in life one's lines never come out quite right at the first performance.

The girl looked at him. She was small, and at the present moment had that air of the floweret surprised while shrinking which adds a good thirty-three per cent to a girl's attractions. Her nose, he noted, was delicately tip-tilted. A certain pallor added to her beauty. Roland's heart executed the opening steps of a buck-and-wing dance.

'Pardon me,' he went on, 'but you appear to be in trouble. Is there anything I can do for you?'

She looked at him again – a keen look which seemed to get into Roland's soul and walk about it with a search-light. Then, as if satisfied by the inspection, she spoke.

'No, I don't think there is,' she said, 'unless you happen to be the proprietor of a weekly paper with a Woman's Page, and need an editress for it.'

'I don't understand.'

'Well, that's all anyone could do for me: give me back my work or give me something else of the same sort.'

'Oh, have you lost your job?'

'I have. So would you mind going away, because I want to go on crying, and I do it better alone! You won't mind my turning you out, I hope, but I was here first, and there are heaps of other benches.'

'No, but wait a minute. I want to hear about this. I might be able – what I mean is – think of something. Tell me all about it.'

There is no doubt that the possession of two hundred and fifty thousand pounds tones down a diffident man's diffidence. Roland began to feel almost masterful.

'Why should I?'

'Why shouldn't you?'

'There's something in that,' said the girl, reflectively. 'After all, you might know somebody. Well, as you want to know, I have just been discharged from a paper called *Squibs*. I used to edit the Woman's Page.'

'By Jove, did you write that article on "Men Who Speak—"?'

The hard manner in which she had wrapped herself as in a garment vanished instantly. Her eyes softened. She even blushed.

'You don't mean to say you read it? I didn't think anyone read *Squibs*.'

'Read it!' cried Roland, recklessly abandoning truth. 'I should jolly well think so. I know it by heart. Do you mean to say that after an article like that, they sacked you?'

'Oh, they didn't send me away for incompetence. It was simply because they couldn't afford to keep me on. Mr Petheram was very nice about it.'

'Who's Mr Petheram?'

A slight twinge – it would be exaggeration to call it jealousy – disturbed Roland's enjoyment of the conversation. Somehow he did not like the idea of this girl being on speaking terms with other men.

For the first time she smiled.

'Mr Petheram's everything. He calls himself the editor, but he's really everything except office-boy, and I expect he'll be that next week. When I started with the paper there was quite a large staff. But it got whittled down by degrees till there were only Mr Petheram and myself. It was like the crew of the *Nancy Bell*. They got eaten one by one, till I was the only one left. And now I've gone. Mr Petheram is doing the whole paper now.'

'He must be clever.'

'He's a genius.'

'How is it that he can't get anything better to do?' he said.

'He has done lots of better things. He used to be at Carmelite House, but they thought he was too old.'

Roland felt relieved. If this Petheram was an old man he did not so much object to her enthusiasm. He conjured up a picture of a white-haired elder with a fatherly manner.

'Oh, he's old, is he?'

'Twenty-four.'

There was a brief silence. Something in the girl's expression stung Roland. She wore a rapt look, as if she were dreaming of the absent Petheram – confound him! He would show her that Petheram was not the only man worth looking rapt about. He rose.

'Would you mind giving me your address?' he said.

'Why?'

'So that I can communicate with you.'

'Why?'

She spoke quietly, but there was an unpleasant sub-tinkle in her voice, as of one who had a short way with Men Who Communicated with Girls.

'In order,' said Roland, carefully, 'that I may offer you your former employment on *Squibs*. I am going to buy it.'

After all, your man of dash and enterprise, your Napoleon, does have his moments. Without looking at her, he perceived that he had bowled her over completely. Something told him that she was staring at him open-mouthed.

Meanwhile, a voice within him was muttering anxiously, 'I wonder how much this is going to cost?'

'You're going to buy *Squibs*!'

Her voice had fallen away to an awe-struck whisper.

'I am.'

She gulped.

'Well, I think you're wonderful.'

So did Roland.

'Where will a letter find you?' he asked.

'My name is March – Bessie March. I'm living at twenty-seven, Guilford Street.'

'Twenty-seven. Thank you. Good morning. I will communicate with you in due course.'

He raised his hat and walked away. He had only gone a few steps when there was a patter of feet behind him. He turned.

'I – I just wanted to thank you,' she said.

'Not at all,' said Roland. 'Not at all.'

He went on his way tingling with just triumph. Petheram? Who was Petheram? Who, in the name of goodness, was Petheram? He had put Petheram in his proper place, he rather fancied. Petheram, forsooth. Laughable!

A copy of the current number of *Squibs*, purchased at a bookstall, informed him that the offices of the paper were in Fetter Lane. It was evidence of his exalted state of mind that he proceeded thither in a cab.

There might have been space to swing a cat in the editorial sanctum of *Squibs*, but it would have been a near thing. As for the outer office, in which a vacant-faced lad of fifteen received Roland and instructed him to wait while he took his card in to Mr Petheram, it was a mere box. Roland was afraid to expand his chest for fear of bruising it.

The boy returned to say that Mr Petheram would see him.

Mr Petheram was a young man with a mop of hair, spectacles, and an air of almost painful restraint, as if it were only by willpower of a high order that he kept himself from bounding about like a Dervish. He was in his shirt-sleeves, and the table before him was heaped high with papers. Opposite him, evidently in the act of taking his leave, was a comfortable-looking man of middle age, with a red face and a short beard. He left as Roland entered, and Roland was surprised to see Mr Petheram spring to his feet, shake his fist at the closing door, and kick the wall with a vehemence which brought down several inches of discoloured plaster.

'Take a seat,' he said, when he had finished this performance. 'What can I do for you?'

Roland had always imagined that editors in their private offices were less easily approached, and, when approached, more brusque. The fact was that Mr Petheram, whose optimism nothing could quench, had mistaken him for a prospective advertiser.

'I want to buy the paper,' said Roland. He was aware that this was an abrupt way of approaching the subject, but, after all, he did want to buy the paper, so why not say so?

Mr Petheram fizzed in his chair. He glowed with excitement.

'Do you mean to tell me there's a single bookstall in London which has sold out? Great Scot! perhaps they've all sold out! How many did you try?'

'I mean buy the whole paper. Become proprietor, you know.'

Roland felt that he was blushing, and hated himself for it. He ought to be carrying this thing through with an air.

Mr Petheram looked at him blankly.

'Why?' he asked.

'Oh, I don't know,' said Roland. He felt the interview was going all wrong. It lacked a stateliness which this kind of interview should have had.

'Honestly?' said Mr Petheram. 'You aren't pulling my leg?'

Roland nodded. Mr Petheram appeared to struggle with his conscience, and finally to be worsted by it, for his next remarks were limpidly honest.

'Don't you be an ass,' he said. 'You don't know what you're letting yourself in for. Did you see that blighter who went out just now? Did you ever see a man in such a beastly state of robust health? Do you know who he is? That's the fellow we've got to pay five pounds a week to for life.'

'Why?'

'We can't get rid of him. When the paper started, the proprietors – not the present ones – thought it would give the thing a boom if they had a football competition with a first prize of a fiver a week for life. Well, that's the man who won it. He's been handed down as a legacy from proprietor to proprietor, till now we've got him. Ages ago they tried to get him to compromise for a lump sum down, but he wouldn't. Said he would only spend it, and preferred to get it by the week. Well, by the time we've paid that vampire, there isn't much left out of our profits. That's why we are at present a little understaffed.'

A frown clouded Mr Petheram's brow. Roland wondered if he was thinking of Bessie March.

'I know all about that,' he said.

'And you still want to buy the thing?'

'Yes.'

'But what on earth for? Mind you, I ought not to be crabbing my own paper, but you seem a good chap, and I don't want to see you landed. Why are you doing it?'

'Oh, just for fun.'

'Ah, now you're talking. If you can afford expensive amusements, go ahead.'

He put his feet on the table and lit a short pipe. His gloomy views on the subject of *Squibs* gave way to a wave of optimism.

'You know,' he said, 'there's really a lot of life in the old rag yet, if it were properly run. What has hampered us has been lack of capital. We haven't been able to advertise. I'm bursting with ideas for booming the paper, only naturally you can't do it for nothing. As for editing, what I don't know about editing – but perhaps you had got somebody else in your mind?'

'No, no,' said Roland, who would not have known an editor from an office-boy. The thought of interviewing prospective editors appalled him.

'Very well, then,' resumed Mr Petheram, reassured, kicking over a heap of papers to give more room for his feet. 'Take it that I continue as editor. We can discuss terms later. Under the present *régime* I have been doing all the work in exchange for a happy home. I suppose you won't want to spoil the ship for a ha'porth of tar? In other words, you would sooner have a happy, well-fed editor running about the place than a broken-down wreck who might swoon from starvation?'

'But one moment,' said Roland. 'Are you sure that the present proprietors will want to sell?'

'Want to sell!' cried Mr Petheram, enthusiastically. 'Why, if they know you want to buy you've as much chance of getting away from them without the paper as – as – well, I can't think of anything that has such a poor chance of anything. If you aren't quick on your feet, they'll cry on your shoulder. Come along, and we'll round them up now.'

He struggled into his coat and gave his hair an impatient brush with a notebook.

'There's just one other thing,' said Roland. 'I have been a regular reader of *Squibs* for some time, and I particularly admire the way in which the Woman's Page—'

'You mean you want to re-engage the editress? Rather. You couldn't do better. I was going to suggest it myself. Now, come along quick before you change your mind or wake up.'

Within a very few days of becoming sole proprietor of *Squibs* Roland began to feel much as a man might who, a novice at the art of steering cars, should find himself at the wheel of a runaway motor. Young Mr Petheram had spoken nothing less than the truth when he had said that he was full of ideas for booming the paper. The infusion of capital into the business acted on him like a powerful stimulant. He exuded ideas at every pore.

Roland's first notion had been to engage a staff of contributors. He was under the impression that contributors were the life-blood of a weekly journal. Mr Petheram corrected this view. He consented to the purchase of a lurid serial story, but that was the last concession he made. Nobody could accuse Mr Petheram of lack of energy. He was willing, even anxious, to write the whole paper himself, with the exception of the Woman's Page, now brightly conducted once more by Miss March. What he wanted Roland to concentrate himself upon was the supplying of capital for ingenious advertising schemes.

'How would it be,' he asked one morning (he always began his remarks with 'How would it be?'), 'if we paid a man to walk down Piccadilly in white-skin tights with the word "*Squibs*" painted in red letters across his chest?'

Roland thought it would certainly not be.

'Good, sound advertising stunt,' urged Mr Petheram. 'You don't like it? All right. You're the boss. Well, how would it be to have a squad of men dressed as Zulus with white shields bearing the legend "*Squibs*"? See what I mean? Have them sprinting along the Strand shouting "Wah, wah, wah! Buy it! Buy it!" It would make people talk.'

Roland emerged from these interviews with his skin crawling with modest apprehension. His was a retiring nature, and the thought of Zulus sprinting down the Strand shouting 'Wah, wah, wah! Buy it! Buy it!' with reference to his personal property appalled him.

He was beginning now heartily to regret having bought the paper, as he generally regretted every definite step which he took. The glow of romance which had sustained him during the preliminary negotiations had faded entirely. A girl has to be possessed of unusual charm to continue to activate B. when she makes it plain daily that her heart is the exclusive property of A.; and Roland had long since ceased to cherish any delusion that

Bessie March was ever likely to feel anything but a mild liking for him. Young Mr Petheram had obviously staked out an indisputable claim. Her attitude towards him was that of an affectionate devotee towards a high priest. One morning, entering the office unexpectedly, Roland found her kissing the top of Mr Petheram's head; and from that moment his interest in the fortunes of *Squibs* sank to zero. It amazed him that he could even have been idiot enough to have allowed himself to be entangled in this insane venture for the sake of an insignificant-looking bit of a girl with a snub nose and a poor complexion.

What particularly galled him was the fact that he was throwing away good cash for nothing. It was true that his capital was more than equal to the on-the-whole modest demands of the paper, but that did not alter the fact that he was wasting money. Mr Petheram always talked buoyantly about turning the corner, but the corner always seemed just as far off.

The old idea of flight, to which he invariably had recourse in any crisis, came upon Roland with irresistible force. He packed a bag, and went to Paris. There, in the discomforts of life in a foreign country, he contrived for a month to forget his white elephant.

He returned by the evening train which deposits the traveller in London in time for dinner.

Strangely enough, nothing was farther from Roland's mind than his bright weekly paper, as he sat down to dine in a crowded grill-room near Piccadilly Circus. Four weeks of acute torment in a city where nobody seemed to understand the simplest English sentence had driven *Squibs* completely from his mind.

The fact that such a paper existed was brought home to him with the coffee. A note was placed upon his table by the attentive waiter.

'What's this?' he asked.

'The lady, sare,' said the waiter, vaguely.

Roland looked round the room excitedly. The spirit of romance gripped him. There were many ladies present, for this particular restaurant was a favourite with artistes who were permitted to 'book in' at their theatres as late as eight-thirty. None of them looked particularly self-conscious, yet one of them had sent him this quite unsolicited tribute. He tore open the envelope.

The message, written in a flowing feminine hand, was brief, and Mrs Grundy herself could have taken no exception to it.

'*Squibs*, one penny weekly, buy it,' it ran.

All the mellowing effects of a good dinner passed away from Roland. He was feverishly irritated. He paid his bill, and left the place.

A visit to a neighbouring music-hall occurred to him as a suitable sedative. Hardly had his nerves ceased to quiver sufficiently to allow him to begin to enjoy the performance, when, in the interval between two of the turns, a man rose in one of the side boxes.

'Is there a doctor in the house?'

There was a hush in the audience. All eyes were directed towards the box. A man in the stalls rose, blushing, and cleared his throat.

'My wife has fainted,' continued the speaker. 'She has just discovered that she has lost her copy of *Squibs*.'

The audience received the statement with the bovine stolidity of an English audience in the presence of the unusual. Not so Roland. Even as the purposeful-looking chuckers-out wended their leopard-like steps towards the box, he was rushing out into the street.

As he stood cooling his indignation in the pleasant breeze

which had sprung up, he was aware of a dense crowd proceeding towards him. It was headed by an individual who shone out against the drab background like a good deed in a naughty world. Nature hath framed strange fellows in her time, and this was one of the strangest that Roland's bulging eyes had ever rested upon. He was a large, stout man, comfortably clad in a suit of white linen, relieved by a scarlet '*Squibs*' across the bosom. His top-hat, at least four sizes larger than any top-hat worn out of a pantomime, flaunted the same word in letters of flame. His umbrella, which, though the weather was fine, he carried open above his head, bore the device, 'One Penny Weekly.'

The arrest of this person by a vigilant policeman and Roland's dive into a taxi-cab occurred simultaneously. Roland was blushing all over. His head was in a whirl. He took the evening paper handed in through the window of the cab quite mechanically, and it was only the strong exhortations of the vendor which eventually induced him to pay for it. This he did with a sovereign, and the cab drove off.

He was just thinking of going to bed several hours later, when it occurred to him that he had not read his paper. He glanced at the first page. The middle column was devoted to a really capitally written account of the proceedings at Bow Street consequent upon the arrest of six men who, it was alleged, had caused a crowd to collect to the disturbance of the peace by parading the Strand in the undress of Zulu warriors, shouting in unison the words, 'Wah, wah, wah! Buy *Squibs*!'

Young Mr Petheram greeted Roland with a joyous enthusiasm which the hound Argus, on the return of Ulysses, might have equalled but could scarcely have surpassed. It seemed to be Mr Petheram's considered opinion that God was in His Heaven and all right with the world. Roland's attempts to correct this belief fell on deaf ears.

'Have I seen the advertisements?' he cried, echoing his editor's first question. 'I've seen nothing else.'

'There!' said Mr Petheram, proudly.

'It can't go on.'

'Yes, it can. Don't you worry. I know they're arrested as fast as we send them out, but, bless you, the supply's endless. Ever since the revue boom started and actors were expected to do six different parts in seven minutes, there are platoons of music-hall pros hanging about the Strand, ready to take on any sort of job you offer them. I have a special staff flushing the Bodegas. These fellows love it. It's meat and drink to them to be right in the public eye like that. Makes them feel ten years younger. It's wonderful the talent kicking about. Those Zulus used to have a steady job as the Six Brothers Biff, Society Contortionists. The revue craze killed them professionally. They cried like children when we took them on. By the way, could you put through an expenses cheque before you go? The fines mount up a bit. But don't you worry about that, either. We're coining money. I'll show you the returns in a minute. I told you we should turn the corner. Turned it! Damme, we've whizzed round it on two wheels. Have you had time to see the paper since you got back? No? Then you haven't seen our new Scandal Page – 'We Just Want to Know, You Know.' It's a corker, and it's sent the circulation up like a rocket. Everybody reads *Squibs* now. I was hoping you would come back soon. I wanted to ask you about taking new offices. We're a bit above this sort of thing now.'

Roland, meanwhile, was reading with horrified eyes the alleged corking scandal page. It seemed to him, without exception, the most frightful production he had ever seen. It appalled him.

'This is awful!' he moaned. 'We shall have a hundred libel actions.'

'Oh, no, that's all right. It's all fake stuff, though the public doesn't know it. If you stuck to real scandals you wouldn't get a par a week. A more moral set of blameless wasters than the blighters who constitute modern society you never struck. But it reads all right, doesn't it? Of course, every now and then one does hear something genuine, and then it goes in. For instance, have you heard of Percy Pook, the bookie? I have got a real ripe thing in about Percy this week – the absolute limpid truth. It will make him sit up a bit. There, just under your thumb.'

Roland removed his thumb, and, having read the paragraph in question, started as if he had removed it from a snake. 'But this is bound to mean a libel action!' he cried.

'Not a bit of it,' said Mr Petheram, comfortably. 'You don't know Percy. I won't bore you with his life-history, but take it from me he doesn't rush into a court of law from sheer love of it. You're safe enough.'

But it appeared that Mr Pook, though coy in the matter of cleansing his scutcheon before a judge and jury, was not wholly without weapons of defence and offence. Arriving at the office next day, Roland found a scene of desolation, in the middle of which sat Jimmy, the vacant-faced office-boy.

'He's gorn,' he observed, looking up as Roland entered.

'What do you mean?'

'Mr Petheram. A couple of fellers come in and went through, and there was a uproar inside there, and presently out they come running, and I went in, and there was Mr Petheram on the floor knocked silly, and the furniture all broke, and now 'e's gorn to 'orspital. Those fellers 'ad been putting 'im froo it proper,' concluded Jimmy, with moody relish.

Roland sat down weakly. Silence reigned in the offices of *Squibs*.

It was broken by the arrival of Miss March. Her exclamation of astonishment at the sight of the wrecked room led to a repetition of Jimmy's story.

She vanished on hearing the name of the hospital to which the stricken editor had been removed, and returned an hour later with flashing eyes and a set jaw.

'Aubrey,' she said – it was news to Roland that Mr Petheram's name was Aubrey – 'is very much knocked about, but he is conscious and sitting up and taking nourishment.'

'That's good.'

'In a spoon only.'

'Ah!' said Roland.

'The doctor says he will not be out for a week. Aubrey is certain it was that horrible bookmaker's men who did it, but of course he can prove nothing. But his last words to me were, "Slip it into Percy again this week." He has given me one or two things to mention. I don't understand them, but Aubrey says they will make him wild.'

Roland's flesh crept. The idea of making Mr Pook any wilder than he appeared to be at present horrified him. Panic gave him strength, and he addressed Miss March, who was looking more like a modern Joan of Arc than anything else on earth, firmly.

'Miss March,' he said, 'I realize that this is a crisis, and that we must all do all that we can for the paper, and I am ready to do anything in reason – but I will *not* slip it into Percy. You have seen the effects of slipping it into Percy. What he or his minions will do if we repeat the process I do not care to think.'

'You are afraid?'

'Yes,' said Roland, simply.

Miss March turned on her heel. It was plain that she regarded him as a worm. Roland did not like being regarded as a worm, but it was infinitely better than being regarded as an interesting case by the house-surgeon of a hospital. He belonged to the school of thought which holds that it is better that people should say of you, 'There he goes,' than that they should say, 'How peaceful he looks.'

Thanks to Mr Petheram, there was a sufficient supply of material in hand to enable *Squibs* to run a fortnight on its own momentum. Roland, however, did not know this, and with a view to doing what little he could to help, he informed Miss March that he would write the Scandal Page. It must be added that the offer was due quite as much to prudence as to chivalry. Roland simply did not dare to trust her with the Scandal Page. In her present mood it was not safe. To slip it into Percy would, he felt, be with her the work of a moment.

Literary composition had never been Roland's *forte*. He stared at the white paper and chewed the pencil which should have been marring its whiteness with stinging paragraphs. No sort of idea came to him.

His brow grew damp. What sort of people – except book-makers – did things you could write scandal about? As far as he could ascertain, nobody.

He picked up the morning paper. The name Windleband caught his eye. A kind of pleasant melancholy came over him as he read the paragraph. How long ago it seemed since he had met that genial financier. The paragraph was not particularly interesting. It gave a brief account of some large deal which Mr Windleband was negotiating. Roland did not understand a word of it, but it gave him an idea.

Mr Windleband's financial standing, he knew, was above suspicion. Mr Windleband had made that clear to him during his visit. There could be no possibility of offending Mr Windleband by a paragraph or two about the manners and customs of financiers. Phrases which his kindly host had used during his visit came back to him, and with them inspiration. Within five minutes he had compiled the following:

WE JUST WANT TO KNOW, YOU KNOW.

*Who* is the eminent financier at present engaged upon one of his biggest deals?

*Whether* the public would not be well advised to look a little closer into it before investing their money?

*If* it is not a fact that this gentleman has bought a first-class ticket to the Argentine in case of accidents?

*Whether* he may not have to use it at any moment?

After that it was easy. Ideas came with a rush. By the end of an hour he had completed a Scandal Page of which Mr Petheram himself might have been proud, without a suggestion of slipping it into Percy. He felt that he could go to Mr Pook and say, 'Percy, on your honour as a British bookmaker, have I slipped it into you in any way whatsoever?' And Mr Pook would be compelled to reply, 'You have not.'

Miss March read the proofs of the page and sniffed. But Miss March's blood was up, and she would have sniffed at anything not directly hostile to Mr Pook.

A week later Roland sat in the office of *Squibs*, reading a letter. It had been sent from No. 18A, Bream's Buildings, E.C., but, from

Roland's point of view, it might have come direct from Heaven; for its contents, signed by Harrison, Harrison, Harrison, and Harrison, solicitors, were to the effect that a client of theirs had instructed them to approach him with a view to purchasing the paper. He would not find their client disposed to haggle over terms, so, hoped Messrs Harrison, Harrison, Harrison, and Harrison, in the event of Roland being willing to sell, they could speedily bring matters to a satisfactory conclusion.

Any conclusion which had left him free of *Squibs* without actual pecuniary loss would have been satisfactory to Roland. He had conceived a loathing for his property which not even its steadily-increasing sales could mitigate. He was round at Messrs Harrisons' offices as soon as a taxi could take him there.

The lawyers were for spinning the thing out with guarded remarks and cautious preambles, but Roland's methods of doing business were always rapid.

'This chap,' he said, 'this fellow who wants to buy *Squibs*, what'll he give?'

'That,' began one of the Harrisons, ponderously, 'would, of course, largely depend—'

'I'll take five thousand. Lock, stock, and barrel, including the present staff, an even five thousand. How's that?'

'Five thousand is a large—'

'Take it or leave it.'

'My dear sir, you hold a pistol to our heads. However, I think that our client might consent to the sum you mention.'

'Good. Well directly I get his cheque the thing's his. By the way, who *is* your client?'

Mr Harrison coughed. 'His name,' he said, 'will be familiar to you. He is the eminent financier, Mr Dermot Windleband.'

The Caout-Chouc was drawing all London. Slightly more indecent than the Salome dance, a shade less reticent than Rag-time, it had driven the Tango out of existence. Nobody tangoed now. Nor, indeed, did anybody actually caout-chouc, for the national dance of Paranoya contained three hundred and fifteen recognized steps; but everybody tried to. Caout-Chouc teas were all the rage. At the night-clubs fair women and brave men reeled about the floor under the impression that they were caout-choucing. A new revue, 'Hullo, Caout-Chouc,' had been pro-duced with success. And the pioneer of the dance, the peerless Maraquita, a native Paranoyan, still performed it nightly at the music-hall where she had first broken loose.

The Caout-Chouc fascinated Roland Bleke. Maraquita fasci-nated him more. Of all the women to whom he had lost his heart at first sight, Maraquita had made the firmest impression upon him. She was what is sometimes called a fine woman. She had large, flashing eyes, the physique of a Rugby International forward, and the agility of a cat on hot bricks. There is a period of about fifty steps somewhere in the middle of the three hun-dred and fifteen where the patient, abandoning the comparative decorum of the earlier movements, whizzes about till she looks like a salmon-coloured whirlwind. That was the bit that hit Roland. Night after night he sat in his stage-box, goggling at Maraquita and applauding wildly.

That she was aware of his existence, that he should ever have the unspeakable happiness of getting to know her, never occurred to him. But one night an attendant came up to his box.

'Excuse me, sir, but are you Mr Roland Bleke? The Señorita Maraquita wishes to speak to you.'

He held open the door of the box. The possibility of refusal did not appear to occur to him. Behind the scenes at that theatre it was generally recognized that when the Peerless One wanted a thing, she got it – quick.

They were alone.

With no protective footlights between himself and her, Roland came to the conclusion that he had made a mistake. It was not that she was any less beautiful at the very close quarters imposed by the limits of the dressing-room, but her personality at this close range had a quality which Roland could only define to himself as formidable.

For perhaps a minute and a half Maraquita fixed her compelling eyes on his without uttering a word. Then she broke a painful silence with this leading question:

'You love me, *hein*?'

Roland nodded feebly.

'All men love me,' said the Peerless One, blowing cigarette smoke. 'But I do not mind.'

This attitude struck Roland as distinctly magnanimous.

'When men make love to me, I send them away – so.'

She waved her hand towards the door, and Roland began to feel almost cheerful again. He was to be dismissed with a caution, after all. The woman had a fine, forgiving nature.

'But not you.'

'Not me?'

'No, not you. You are the man I have been waiting for. I read about you in the paper, Señor Bleke. I see your picture in the paper, too. I say to myself, "What a man!"'

'Those picture-paper photographs always make one look rather weird,' mumbled Roland.

'I see you night after night in your box. Poof! I love you.'

'Thanks awfully,' bleated Roland.

'You would do anything for my sake, *hein*?'

Roland felt that he would like to know just what she meant by 'anything,' but Maraquita was one of those orators who do not pause for a reply.

'Ah! I knew it!' she cried. 'I knew you were that kind of man directly I see you. No,' she added, as Roland writhed uneasily in his chair, 'do not embrace me. Later, yes; but now, no. Not till the Great Day.'

What the Great Day might be Roland could not even faintly conjecture. He could only hope that it would also be a remote one.

'And now,' said the señorita, throwing a cloak about her shoulders, 'you come away with me to my house. My friends are there awaiting us. They will be glad and proud to meet you.'

After his first inspection of the house and the friends, Roland came to the conclusion that he preferred Maraquita's room to her company. The former was large and airy. The latter, with one exception, small and hairy. The exception Maraquita addressed as Bombito. He was a conspicuous figure. He was, as the railway-station posters say of Slopton-on-Sea – different. He was one of those outsize, hasty-looking men. One suspected him of carrying lethal weapons.

Maraquita presented Roland to the company. The native speech of Paranoya sounded like shorthand with a blend of

Spanish. An expert could evidently squeeze a good deal of it into a minute. Its effect on the company was good. They were manifestly soothed. Even Bombito.

Introductions in detail then took place. This time, for Roland's benefit, Maraquita spoke in English, and he learned that most of those present were marquesses. One or two outsiders were only counts, but marquesses predominated. Before him, so he gathered from Maraquita, stood the very flower of Paranoya's aristocracy, driven from their native land by the Infamy of '05. Roland was too polite to inquire what on earth the Infamy of '05 might be, but its mention had a marked effect on the company.

Paranoya had, it appeared, existed fairly peacefully for centuries under the rule of the Alejandro dynasty. Then, in the reign of Alejandro XIII, disaffection had begun to spread, culminating in the Infamy of '05, which, Roland had at last discovered, was nothing less than the abolition of the monarchy and the installation of a republic.

These events had been received by the world at large with an equanimity bordering on contempt, but not by the old *noblesse* of Paranoya. Not for them the Republican yoke. Since 1905 the one thing for which they had lived, besides the Caout-Chouc, was to see the monarchy restored and their beloved Alejandro XIII back on his throne. Their efforts towards this end had been untiring, and were at last showing signs of bearing fruit. Paranoya, Maraquita assured Roland, was honeycombed with intrigue. The army was disaffected, the people anxious for a return to the old order of things. A more propitious moment for striking the decisive blow was never likely to arrive. The question was purely one of funds.

At the mention of the word 'funds,' Roland, who had become

thoroughly bored with the lecture on Paranoyan history, sat up and took notice. He had an instinctive feeling that he was about to be called upon for a subscription to the cause of the distressful country's freedom. Especially by Bombito.

He was right. A moment later Maraquita had begun to make a speech. She spoke in Paranoyan, and Roland could not follow her, but he gathered that it somehow had reference to himself. As, at the end of it, the entire company rose to their feet and extended their glasses towards him with a mighty shout, he assumed that Maraquita had been proposing his health.

'They say "To the Liberator of Paranoya,"' kindly translated the Peerless One. 'Ah!' Her fine eyes blazed, as a lugubrious chant succeeded the cheering. 'Now they sing our beloved anthem, the Royal anthem of Paranoya; it has not been heard on Paranoyan soil since the Infamy of '05.'

To Roland it seemed an ample justification for the Infamy of '05.

'You must excuse,' said Maraquita, tolerantly, as a bevy of patriots surrounded Roland and kissed him on the cheek. 'They are so grateful to the saviour of our country. I myself would kiss you, were it not that I have sworn that no man's lips shall touch mine till the Royal Standard floats once more above the palace of Paranoya. But that will be soon. With you on our side we cannot fail.'

What did the woman mean? Roland asked himself wildly. Did she labour under the distressing delusion that he proposed to shed his blood on behalf of a deposed monarch to whom he had never been introduced?

Maraquita's next remarks made the matter clear.

'I have told them,' she said, 'that you love me, that you are willing to risk everything for my sake. I have promised them that you, the rich Señor Bleke, will supply the funds for the revolution. Once more, comrades: "To the Saviour of Paranoya!"'

Roland tried his hardest to catch the infection of this patriotic enthusiasm, but somehow he could not do it. Base, sordid, mercenary speculations would intrude themselves. About how much was a good, well-furnished revolution likely to cost? As delicately as he could, he put the question to Maraquita.

She said, 'Poof! The cost? La, la!'

Which was all very well, but hardly satisfactory as a business chat.

'We will talk of that later,' she went on. 'Now we will enjoy ourselves, isn't it?'

And that was all Roland could get out of her.


The next few days passed for Roland in a sort of dream. It was the kind of dream which it is not easy to distinguish from a nightmare. It amazed him that he had ever wanted to know Maraquita. It is not easy to achieve happiness in this world, but Roland felt that a very fair basis for it could be had simply by not knowing Maraquita. How people who did not know Maraquita could go about the world grumbling was more than he could understand. They did not know their luck.

Her reticence at the supper-party on the subject of details connected with the financial side of revolutions entirely disappeared. She now talked nothing but figures, and from the confused mass which she presented to him Roland was able to gather that, in financing the restoration of Royalty in Paranoya, he would indeed be risking everything for her sake.

In the matter of revolutions Maraquita was no niggard. She knew how the thing should be done – well, or not at all. There would be so much for rifles, machine-guns, and what-not; and there would be so much for the expense of smuggling them into the country. Then there would be so much to be laid out in corrupting the Republican army. Roland brightened a little when they came to this item. As the standing army of Paranoya amounted to twenty thousand men, and as it seemed possible to corrupt it thoroughly at a cost of about thirty shillings a head, the obvious course, to Roland's way of thinking, was to concentrate on this side of the question, and thus avoid unnecessary bloodshed.

It appeared, however, that Maraquita did not want to avoid bloodshed – that she rather liked bloodshed, that the leaders of the revolution would be disappointed if there were no bloodshed. Especially Bombito. Unless, she pointed out, there was a certain amount of carnage, looting, and so on, the revolution would not achieve a popular success. True, the beloved Alejandro might be restored, but he would sit upon a throne that was insecure unless the coronation festivities took a bloodthirsty turn. By all means, said Maraquita, corrupt the army, but not at the risk of making the affair tame and unpopular. Paranoya was an emotional country, and liked its revolutions with a bit of zip to them.

It was about ten days after he had definitely cast in his lot with the revolutionary party that Roland was made aware that these things were a little more complex than he had imagined. He had reconciled himself to the financial outlay. It had been difficult, but he had done it. That his person as well as his purse would be placed in peril he had not foreseen.

The fact was borne in upon him at the end of the second week by the arrival of the deputation.

It blew in from the street just as he was enjoying his after-dinner cigar.

It consisted of three men, one long and suave, the other two short, stout, and silent. They all had the sallow complexion and undue hairiness which he had come by this time to associate with the native of Paranoya.

For a moment he mistook them for a drove of exiled noblemen whom he had not had the pleasure of meeting at the supper-party; and he waited resignedly for them to make night hideous with the Royal anthem. He poised himself on his toes, the more readily to spring aside if they should try to kiss him on the cheek.

'Mr Bleke?' said the long man.

His companions drifted towards the cigar-box which stood open on the table, and looked at it wistfully.

'Long live the monarchy,' said Roland, wearily. He had gathered in the course of his dealings with the exiled ones that this remark generally went well.

On the present occasion it elicited no outburst of cheering. On the contrary, the long man frowned, and his two companions helped themselves to a handful of cigars apiece with a marked moodiness.

'Death to the monarchy,' corrected the long man, coldly. 'And,' he added, with a wealth of meaning in his voice, 'to all who meddle in the affairs of our beloved country and seek to do it harm.'

'I don't know what you mean,' said Roland.

'Yes, Señor Bleke, you do know what I mean. I mean that you will be well advised to abandon the schemes which you are hatching with the malcontents who would do my beloved land an injury.'

The conversation was growing awkward. Roland had got so into the habit of taking it for granted that every Paranoyan he met must of necessity be a devotee of the beloved Alejandro that it came as a shock to him to realize that there were those who objected to his restoration to the throne. Till now he had looked on the enemy as something in the abstract. It had not struck him that the people for whose correction he was buying all these rifles and machine-guns were individuals with a lively distaste for having their blood shed.

'Señor Bleke,' resumed the speaker, frowning at one of his companions whose hand was hovering above the bottle of liqueur brandy, 'you are a man of sense. You know what is safe and what is not safe. Believe me, this scheme of yours is not safe. You have been led away, but there is still time to withdraw. Do so, and all is well. Do not so, and your blood be upon your own head.'

'My *blood*!' gasped Roland.

The speaker bowed.

'That is all,' he said. 'We merely came to give the warning. Ah, Señor Bleke, do not be rash. You think that here, in this great London of yours, you are safe. You look at the policeman upon the corner of the road, and you say to yourself, "I am safe." Believe me, not at all so is it, but much the opposite. We have ways by which it is of no account the policeman on the corner of the road. That is all, Señor Bleke. We wish you a good night.'

The deputation withdrew.

Maraquita, informed of the incident, snapped her fingers and said 'Poof!' It sometimes struck Roland that she would be more real help in a difficult situation if she could get out of the habit of saying 'Poof!'

'It is nothing,' she said.

'No?' said Roland.

'We easily out-trick them, isn't it? You make a will leaving your money to the Cause, and then where are they, *hein*?'

It was one way of looking at it, but it brought little balm to Roland. He said so. Maraquita scanned his face keenly.

'You are not weakening, Roland?' she said. 'You would not betray us now?'

'Well, of course, I don't know about betraying, you know, but still – What I mean is—'

Maraquita's eyes seemed to shoot forth two flames.

'Take care!' she cried. 'With me it is nothing, for I know that your heart is with Paranoya. But if the others once had cause to suspect that your resolve was failing – ah! If Bombito—'

Roland took her point. He had forgotten Bombito for the moment.

'For goodness' sake,' he said, hastily, 'don't go saying anything to Bombito to give him the idea that I'm trying to back out. Of course you can rely on me, and all that. That's all right.'

Maraquita's gaze softened. She raised her glass – they were lunching at the time – and put it to her lips.

'To the Saviour of Paranoya!' she said.

'Beware!' whispered a voice in Roland's ear.

He turned with a start. A waiter was standing behind him, a small, dark, hairy man. He was looking into the middle distance with the abstracted air which waiters cultivate. Roland stared at him, but he did not move.

That evening, returning to his flat, Roland was paralysed by the sight of the word 'Beware!' scrawled across the mirror in his bedroom. It had apparently been done with a diamond. He rang the bell.

'Sir?' said the competent valet. ('Competent valets are in attendance at each of these flats.' – Advt.)

'Has anyone been in here since I left?'

'Yes, sir. A foreign-looking gentleman called. He said he knew you, sir. I showed him in, as he said he would wait.'

The same night, well on in the small hours, the telephone-bell rang. Roland dragged himself out of bed.

'Halloa?'

'Is that Señor Bleke?'

'Yes. What is it?'

'Beware!'

Things were becoming intolerable. Roland had a certain amount of nerve, but not enough to enable him to bear up against this sinister persecution. Yet what could he do? Suppose he did beware, to the extent of withdrawing his support from the Royalist movement, what then? Bombito! If ever there was a toad under the harrow, he was that toad. And all because a perfectly respectful admiration for the Caout-Chouc had led him to occupy a stage-box several nights in succession at the theatre where the peerless Maraquita tied herself into knots at a salary of two hundred pounds a week. It was hard.

A few days later somebody shot a bullet through the window of his sitting-room. He was out at the time, but the incident had the effect of putting the final touch to his gloom.

There was an air of unusual excitement in Maraquita's manner at their next meeting.

'We have been in communication with Him,' she whispered. 'He will receive you. He will give an audience to the Saviour of Paranoya.'

'Eh? Who will?'

'Our beloved Alejandro. He wishes to see his faithful servant. We are to go to him at once.'

'Where?'

'At his own house. He will receive you in person.'

Such was the quality of the emotions through which he had been passing of late that Roland felt but a faint interest at the prospect of meeting face to face a genuine – if exiled – monarch.

The cab drew up at a gloomy-looking house in a fashionable square. Roland rang the doorbell. There seemed a certain element of the prosaic in the action. He wondered what he should say to the butler. 'Is the King at home?' was banal.

There was, however, no need for words. The door opened, and they were ushered in without parley. A butler and two footmen showed them into a luxuriously-furnished ante-room. Roland entered with two thoughts running in his mind. The first was that the beloved Alejandro had got an uncommonly snug crib; the second that this was exactly like going to see the dentist.

Presently the squad of retainers returned, the butler leading.

'His Majesty will receive Mr Bleke.'

Roland followed him with tottering knees.

His Majesty King Alejandro XIII on the retired list was a genial-looking man of middle age, comfortably stout about the middle and a little bald as to the forehead. He might have been a prosperous stockbroker. Roland felt more at his ease at the very sight of him.

'Sit down, Mr Bleke,' said His Majesty, as the door closed. 'I have been wanting to see you for some time.'

Roland had nothing to say. He was regaining his composure, but he had a long way to go yet before he could feel thoroughly at home.

King Alejandro produced a cigarette-case and offered it to Roland, who shook his head speechlessly. The King lit a cigarette, and smoked thoughtfully for a while.

'You know, Mr Bleke,' he said at last, 'this must stop. It really must. I mean, your devoted efforts on my behalf.'

Roland gaped at him.

'You are a very young man. I had expected to see someone much older. Your youth gives me the impression that you have gone into this affair from a spirit of adventure. I can assure you that you have nothing to gain commercially by interfering with my late kingdom. I hope, before we part, that I can persuade you to abandon your idea of financing this movement to restore me to the throne.'

'I don't understand – er – your Majesty.'

'I will explain. Please treat what I shall say as strictly confidential. You must know, Mr Bleke, that these attempts to re-establish me as a reigning monarch in Paranoya are, frankly, the curse of an otherwise very pleasant existence. You look surprised! My dear sir, do you *know* Paranoya? Have you ever been there? Have you the remotest idea what sort of life a King of Paranoya leads? I have tried it, and I can assure you that a coal-heaver is happy by comparison. In the first place, the climate of the country is abominable. I always had a cold in the head. Secondly, there is a small but energetic section of the populace whose sole recreation it seems to be to use their monarch as a target for bombs. They are not very good bombs, it is true – the science of chemistry is in its infancy in Paranoya – but one in, say, ten explodes, and even an occasional bomb is unpleasant if you are the target. Finally, I am much too fond of your delightful country to wish to leave it. I was educated in England – I am a Magdalen man – and I have the greatest horror of ever being compelled to leave it. My present life suits me exactly. There is no pomp, no ridiculous ceremony, nothing but quiet enjoyment. Can you wonder that I do not rejoice when well-meaning but officious persons try to drive me from London to a very depressing and unhealthy existence in my native country? That is all I wished to say, Mr Bleke. For both our sakes, for the sake of my comfort and your purse, abandon this scheme of yours.'

Roland walked home thoughtfully. Maraquita had left the Royal residence long before he had finished the whiskey-and-soda which the genial monarch had pressed upon him. As he walked, the futility of his situation came home to him more and more. Whatever he did, he was bound to displease somebody; and these Paranoyans were so confoundedly impulsive when they were vexed.

For two days he avoided Maraquita. On the third, with something of the instinct which draws the murderer to the spot where he has buried the body, he called at her house.

She was not present, but otherwise there was a full gathering. There were the marquesses, the counts, and also Bombito.

He looked unhappily round the crowd.

Somebody gave him a glass of champagne. He raised it.

'To the revolution,' he said, mechanically.

There was a silence – it seemed to Roland an awkward silence. As if he had said something improper, the marquesses and counts began to drift from the room, till only Bombito was left. Roland regarded him with some apprehension. He was looking larger and more unusual than ever.

But tonight, apparently, Bombito was in genial mood. He came forward and slapped Roland on the shoulder. And then the remarkable fact came to light that Bombito spoke English, or a sort of English.

'My old chap,' he said. 'I would have a speech with you.'

He slapped Roland again on the shoulder.

'The others they say, "Break it with Señor Bleke gently."

Maraquita say, "Break it with Señor Bleke gently." So I break it with you gently.'

He dealt Roland a third stupendous punch. Whatever was to be broken gently, it was plain to Roland that it was not himself. And suddenly there came to him a sort of intuition that told him that Bombito was nervous.

'After all you have done for us, Señor Bleke, we shall seem to you ver' ungrateful bounders, but what is it? Yes? No? I shouldn't wonder, perhaps. The whole fact is that there has been political crisis in Paranoya. Upset. Apple-cart. Yes? You follow? No? The Ministry have been – what do you say? – put through it. Expelled. Broken up. No more Ministry. New Ministry wanted. To conciliate Royalist party, that is the cry. So deputation of leading persons, good chaps, prominent merchants and that sort of bounder, call upon us. They offer me to be President. See? No? Yes? That's right. I am ambitious blighter, Señor Bleke. What about it, no? I accept. I am new President of Paranoya. So no need for your kind assistance. Royalist revolution up the spout. No more Royalist revolution.'

The wave of relief which swept over Roland ebbed sufficiently after an interval to enable him to think of someone but himself. He was not fond of Maraquita, but he had a tender heart, and this, he felt, would kill the poor girl.

'But Maraquita—?'

'That's all right, splendid old chap. No need to worry about Maraquita, stout old boy. Where the husband goes, so does the wife go. As you say, whither thou goes will I follow, no?'

'But I don't understand. Maraquita is not your wife?'

'Why, certainly, old heart. What else?'

'Have you been married to her all the time?'

'Why, certainly, good dear boy.'

The room swam before Roland's eyes. There was no place in his mind for meditations on the perfidy of woman. He groped forward and found Bombito's hand.

'By Jove,' he said, thickly, as he wrung it again and again, 'I knew you were a good sort the first time I saw you. Have a drink or something. Have a cigar or something. Have something, anyway, and sit down and tell me all about it.'

'What do you mean – you can't marry him after all? After all what? Why can't you marry him? You are perfectly childish.'

Lord Evenwood's gentle voice, which had in its time lulled the House of Peers to slumber more often than any voice ever heard in the Gilded Chamber, had in it a note of unwonted but quite justifiable irritation. If there was one thing more than another that Lord Evenwood disliked, it was any interference with arrangements already made.

'The man,' he continued, 'is not unsightly. The man is not conspicuously vulgar. The man does not eat peas with his knife. The man pronounces his aitches with meticulous care and accuracy. The man, moreover, is worth rather more than a quarter of a million pounds. I repeat, you are childish.'

'Yes, I know he's a very decent little chap, father,' said Lady Eva. 'It's not that at all.'

'I should be gratified, then, to hear what, in your opinion, it is.'

'Well, *do* you think I could be happy with him?'

Lady Kimbuck gave tongue. She was Lord Evenwood's sister. She spent a very happy widowhood interfering in the affairs of the various branches of her family.

'We're not asking you to be happy. You have such odd ideas of happiness. Your idea of happiness is to be married to your cousin Gerry, whose only visible means of support, so far as I can gather, is the four hundred a year which he draws as a member for a constituency which has every intention of throwing him out at the next election.'

Lady Eva blushed. Lady Kimbuck's faculty for nosing out the secrets of her family had made her justly disliked from the Hebrides to Southern Cornwall.

'Young O'Rion is not to be thought of,' said Lord Evenwood, firmly. 'Not for an instant. Apart from anything else, his politics are all wrong. Moreover, you are engaged to this Mr Bleke. It is a sacred responsibility not lightly to be evaded. You cannot pledge your word one day to enter upon the most solemn contract known to – ah – the civilized world, and break it the next. It is not fair to the man. It is not fair to me. You know that all I live for is to see you comfortably settled. If I could myself do anything for you, the matter would be different. But these abominable land taxes and Blowick – especially Blowick – no, no, it's out of the question. You will be very sorry if you do anything foolish. I can assure you that Roland Blekes are not to be found – ah – on every bush. Men are extremely shy of marrying nowadays.'

'Especially,' said Lady Kimbuck, 'into a family like ours. What with Blowick's scandal, and that shocking business of your grandfather and the circus-woman, to say nothing of your poor father's trouble in 'eighty-five—'

'Thank you, Sophia,' interrupted Lord Evenwood, hurriedly. 'It is unnecessary to go into all that now. Suffice it that there are adequate reasons, apart from all moral obligations, why Eva should not break her word to Mr Bleke.'

Lady Kimbuck's encyclopædic grip of the family annals was a source of the utmost discomfort to her relatives. It was known that more than one firm of publishers had made her tempting offers for her reminiscences, and the family looked on like nervous spectators at a battle while Cupidity fought its ceaseless fight with Laziness; for the Evenwood family had at various times and in various ways stimulated the circulation of the evening papers. Most of them were living down something, and it was Lady Kimbuck's habit, when thwarted in her lightest whim, to retire to her boudoir and announce that she was not to be disturbed, as she was at last making a start on her book. Abject surrender followed on the instant.

At this point in the discussion she folded up her crochet-work and rose.

'It is absolutely necessary for you, my dear, to make a good match, or you will all be ruined. I, of course, can always support my declining years with literary work, but—'

Lady Eva groaned. Against this last argument there was no appeal.

Lady Kimbuck patted her affectionately on the shoulder.

'There, run along now,' she said. 'I dare say you've got a headache or something that made you say a lot of foolish things you didn't mean. Go down to the drawing-room. I expect Mr Bleke is waiting there to say good night to you. I am sure he must be getting quite impatient.'

Down in the drawing-room Roland Bleke was hoping against hope that Lady Eva's prolonged absence might be due to the fact that she had gone to bed with a headache, and that he might escape the nightly interview which he so dreaded.

Reviewing his career, as he sat there, Roland came to the conclusion that women had the knack of affecting him with a form of temporary insanity. They temporarily changed his whole nature. They made him feel for a brief while that he was a dashing young man, capable of the highest flights of love. It was only later that the reaction came and he realized that he was nothing of the sort. At heart he was afraid of women, and in the entire list of the women of whom he had been afraid he could not find one who had terrified him so much as Lady Eva Blyton.

Other women – notably Maraquita, now happily helping to direct the destinies of Paranoya – had frightened him by their individuality. Lady Eva frightened him both by her individuality and the atmosphere of aristocratic exclusiveness which she conveyed. He had no idea whatever of what was the proper procedure for a man engaged to the daughter of an earl. Daughters of earls had been to him till now mere names in the society columns of the morning paper. The very rules of the game were beyond him. He felt like a confirmed Association footballer suddenly called upon to play in an international Rugby match.

All along, from the very moment when – to his unbounded astonishment – she had accepted him, he had known that he was making a mistake; but he never realized it with such painful clearness as he did this evening. He was filled with a sort of blind terror. He cursed the fate which had taken him to the charity bazaar at which he had first come under the notice of Lady Kimbuck. The fatuous snobbishness which had made him leap at her invitation to spend a few days at Evenwood Towers he regretted; but for that he blamed himself less. Further acquaintance with Lady Kimbuck had convinced him that if she had wanted him she would have got him somehow, whether he had accepted or refused.

What he really blamed himself for was his mad proposal. There had been no need for it. True, Lady Eva had created a riot of burning emotions in his breast from the moment when they met; but he should have had the sense to realize that she was not the right mate for him, even though he might have a quarter of a million tucked away in gilt-edged securities. Their lives could not possibly mix. He was a commonplace young man with a fondness for the pleasures of the people. He liked cheap papers, picture-palaces, and Association football. Merely to think of Association football in connection with her was enough to make the folly of his conduct clear. He ought to have been content to worship her from afar as some inaccessible goddess.

A light step outside the door made his heart stop beating.

'I've just looked in to say good night, Mr – er – Roland,' she said, holding out her hand. 'Do excuse me. I've got such a headache.'

'Oh, yes; rather. I'm awfully sorry.'

If there was one person in the world Roland despised and hated at that moment, it was himself.

'Are you going out with the guns tomorrow?' asked Lady Eva, languidly.

'Oh, yes; rather. I mean, no. I'm afraid I don't shoot.'

The back of his neck began to glow. He had no illusions about himself. He was the biggest ass in Christendom.

'Perhaps you'd like to play a round of golf, then?'

'Oh, yes; rather. I mean, no.' There it was again, that awful phrase. He was certain he had not intended to utter it. She must be thinking him a perfect lunatic. 'I don't play golf.'

They stood looking at each other for a moment. It seemed to Roland that her gaze was partly contemptuous, partly pitying. He longed to tell her that, though she had happened to pick on his weak points in the realm of sport, there were things he could do. An insane desire came upon him to babble about his school football team. Should he ask her to feel his quite respectable biceps? No.

'Never mind,' she said, kindly. 'I dare say we shall think of something to amuse you.'

She held out her hand again. He took it in his for the briefest possible instant, painfully conscious the while that his own hand was clammy from the emotion through which he had been passing.

'Good night.'

'Good night.'

Thank Heaven she was gone. That let him out for another twelve hours at least.

A quarter of an hour later found Roland still sitting where she had left him, his head in his hands. The groan of an overwrought soul escaped him.

'I can't do it!'

He sprang to his feet.

'I won't do it!'

A smooth voice from behind him spoke.

'I think you are quite right, sir – if I may make the remark.'

Roland had hardly ever been so startled in his life. In the first place, he was not aware of having uttered his thoughts aloud; in the second, he had imagined that he was alone in the room. And so, a moment before, he had been. But the owner of the voice possessed, among other qualities, the cat-like faculty of entering a room perfectly noiselessly – a fact which had won for him, in the course of a long career in the service of the best families, the flattering position of star witness in a number of England's raciest divorce cases.

Mr Teal, the butler – for it was no less a celebrity who had broken in on Roland's reverie – was a long, thin man of a some- what priestly cast of countenance. He lacked that air of reproving hauteur which many butlers possess, and it was for this reason that Roland had felt drawn to him during the black days of his stay at Evenwood Towers. Teal had been uncommonly nice to him on the whole. He had seemed to Roland, stricken by interviews with his host and Lady Kimbuck, the only human thing in the place.

He liked Teal. On the other hand, Teal was certainly taking a liberty. He could, if he so pleased, tell Teal to go to the devil. Technically he had the right to freeze Teal with a look.

He did neither of these things. He was feeling very lonely and very forlorn in a strange and depressing world, and Teal's voice and manner were soothing.

'Hearing you speak, and seeing nobody else in the room,' went on the butler, 'I thought for a moment that you were addressing me.'

This was not true, and Roland knew it was not true. Instinct told him that Teal knew that he knew it was not true; but he did not press the point.

'What do you mean – you think I am quite right?' he said. 'You don't know what I was thinking about.'

Teal smiled indulgently.

'On the contrary, sir. A child could have guessed it. You have just come to the decision – in my opinion a thoroughly sensible one – that your engagement to her ladyship cannot be allowed to go on. You are quite right, sir. It won't do.'

Personal magnetism covers a multitude of sins. Roland was perfectly well aware that he ought not to be standing here chatting over his and Lady Eva's intimate affairs with a butler; but such was Teal's magnetism that he was quite unable to do the right thing and tell him to mind his own business. 'Teal, you forget yourself,' would have covered the situation. Roland, however, was physically incapable of saying, 'Teal, you forget yourself.' The bird knows all the time that he ought not to stand talking to the snake, but he is incapable of ending the conversation. Roland was conscious of a momentary wish that he was the sort of man who could tell butlers that they forgot themselves. But then that sort of man would never be in this sort of trouble. The 'Teal-you-forget-yourself' type of man would be a first-class shot, a plus golfer, and would certainly consider himself extremely lucky to be engaged to Lady Eva.

'The question is,' went on Mr Teal, 'how are we to break it off?'

Roland felt that, as he had sinned against all the decencies in allowing the butler to discuss his affairs with him, he might just as well go the whole hog and allow the discussion to run its course. And it was an undeniable relief to talk about the infernal thing to someone.

He nodded gloomily and committed himself. Teal resumed his remarks with the gusto of a fellow-conspirator.

'It's not an easy thing to do gracefully, sir; believe me, it isn't. And it's got to be done gracefully, or not at all. You can't go to her ladyship and say, "It's all off, and so am I," and catch the next train for London. The rupture must be of her ladyship's making. If some fact, some disgraceful information, concerning you were to come to her ladyship's ears, that would be a simple way out of the difficulty.'

He eyed Roland meditatively.

'If, for instance, you had ever been in jail, sir?'

'Well, I haven't.'

'No offence intended, sir, I'm sure. I merely remembered that you had made a great deal of money very quickly. My experience of gentlemen who have made a great deal of money very quickly is that they had generally done their bit of time. But, of course, if you— Let me think. Do you drink, sir?'

'No.'

Mr Teal sighed. Roland could not help feeling that he was disappointing the old man a good deal.

'You do not, I suppose, chance to have a past?' asked Mr Teal, not very hopefully. 'I use the word in its technical sense. A deserted wife? Some poor creature you have treated shamefully?'

At the risk of sinking still farther in the butler's esteem, Roland was compelled to answer in the negative.

'I was afraid not,' said Mr Teal, shaking his head. 'Thinking it all over yesterday, I said to myself, "I'm afraid he wouldn't have one." You don't look like the sort of gentleman who had done much with his time.'

'Thinking it over?'

'Not on your account, sir,' explained Mr Teal. 'On the family's. I disapproved of this match from the first. A man who has served a family as long as I have had the honour of serving his lordship's comes to entertain a high regard for the family prestige. And, with no offence to yourself, sir, this would not have done.'

'Well, it looks as if it would have to do,' said Roland, gloomily. 'I can't see any way out of it.'

'I can, sir. My niece at Aldershot.'

Mr Teal wagged his head at him with a kind of priestly archness.

'You cannot have forgotten my niece at Aldershot?'

Roland stared at him dumbly. It was like a line out of a melodrama. He feared, first for his own, then for the butler's sanity. The latter was smiling gently, as one who sees light in a difficult situation.

'I've never been at Aldershot in my life.'

'For our purposes you have sir. But I'm afraid I am puzzling you. Let me explain. I've got a niece over at Aldershot. I am sure she would do it for a consideration.'

'Do what?'

'Be your past, sir. Dyed yellow hair, sir,' he went on, with enthusiasm, 'done all frizzy. You couldn't find a better if you tried for a twelvemonth.'

'But, I say—!'

'I suppose a hundred wouldn't hurt you?'

'Well, no, I suppose not; but—'

'Then put the whole thing in my hands, sir. I'll ask leave off tomorrow and pop over and see her. I'll arrange for her to come here the day after to see you. Leave it all to me. Tonight you must write the letters.'

'Letters?'

'Naturally there would be letters, sir. It is an inseparable feature of these cases.'

'Do you mean that I have got to write to her? But I shouldn't know what to say. I've never seen her.'

'That will be quite all right, sir, if you place yourself in my hands. I will come to your room after everybody's gone to bed and help you write those letters. You have some note-paper with your own address on it? Then it will all be perfectly simple.'

When, some hours later, he read over the ten or twelve exceedingly passionate epistles which, with the butler's assistance, he had succeeded in writing to Miss Maud Chilvers, Roland came to the conclusion that there must have been a time when Mr Teal was a good deal less respectable than he appeared to be at present. Byronic was the only adjective applicable to his collaborator's style of amatory composition. In every letter there were passages against which Roland had felt compelled to make a modest protest.

'"A thousand kisses on your lovely rose-bud of a mouth." Don't you think that is a little too warmly coloured? And, "I am languishing for the pressure of your ivory arms about my neck and the sweep of your silken hair against my cheek." What I mean is – well, what about it, you know?'

'The phrases,' said Mr Teal, not without a touch of displeasure, 'to which you take exception are taken bodily from correspondence (which I happened to have the advantage of perusing) addressed by the late Lord Evenwood to Animalcula, Queen of the High Wire at Astley's Circus. His lordship, I may add, was considered an authority in these matters.'

Roland criticized no more. He handed over the letters, which, at Mr Teal's direction, he had headed with various dates, covering roughly a period of about two months antecedent to his arrival at the Towers.

'That,' Mr Teal explained, 'will make your conduct definitely unpardonable. With this woman's kisses hot on your lips' – Mr Teal was still slightly aglow with the fire of inspiration – 'you have the effrontery to come here and offer yourself to her ladyship.'

With Roland's timid suggestion that it was perhaps a mistake to overdo the atmosphere, the butler found himself unable to agree.

'You can't make yourself out too bad. If you don't pitch it hot and strong, her ladyship might quite likely forgive you. Then where would you be?'

Miss Maud Chilvers, of Aldershot, burst into Roland's life like one of the shells of her native heath two days later at about five in the afternoon.

It was an entrance which any stage-manager might have been proud of having arranged. The lighting, the grouping, the lead-up – all were perfect. The family had just finished tea in the long drawing-room. Lady Kimbuck was crocheting, Lord Evenwood dozing, Lady Eva reading, and Roland thinking. A peaceful scene.

A soft, rippling murmur, scarcely to be reckoned a snore, had just proceeded from Lord Evenwood's parted lips, when the door opened, and Teal announced:

'Miss Chilvers.'

Roland stiffened in his chair. Now that the ghastly moment had come, he felt too petrified with fear even to act the little part in which he had been diligently rehearsed by the obliging Mr Teal. He simply sat and did nothing.

It was speedily made clear to him that Miss Chilvers would do all the actual doing that was necessary. The butler had drawn no false picture of her personal appearance. Dyed yellow hair done all frizzy was but one facet of her many-sided impossibilities. In the serene surroundings of the long drawing-room she looked more unspeakable than Roland had ever imagined her. With such a leading lady his drama could not fail of success. He should have been pleased; he was merely appalled. The thing might have a happy ending, but while it lasted it was going to be terrible.

She had a flatteringly attentive reception. Nobody failed to notice her. Lord Evenwood woke with a start, and stared at her as if she had been some ghost from his trouble of 'eighty-five. Lady Eva's face expressed sheer amazement. Lady Kimbuck, laying down her crochet-work, took one look at the apparition, and instantly decided that one of her numerous erring relatives had been at it again. Of all the persons in the room she was possibly the only one completely cheerful. She was used to these situations and enjoyed them. Her mind, roaming into the past, recalled the night when her cousin Warminster had been pinked by a stiletto in his own drawing-room by a lady from South America. Happy days, happy days!

Lord Evenwood had by this time come to the conclusion that the festive Blowick must be responsible for this visitation. He rose with dignity.

'To what are we——?' he began.

Miss Chilvers, resolute young woman, had no intention of standing there while other people talked. She shook her gleaming head and burst into speech.

'Oh, yes; I know I've no right to be coming walking in here among a lot of perfect strangers at their teas, but what I say is, "Right's right and wrong's wrong all the world over," and I may be poor, but I have my feelings. No, thank you, I won't sit down. I've not come for the weekend, I've come to say a few words, and when I've said them I'll go, and not before. A lady friend of mine happened to be reading her *Daily Sketch* the other day, and she said, "Halloa, halloa!" and passed it on to me with her thumb on a picture which had under it that it was Lady Eva Blyton, who was engaged to be married to Mr Roland Bleke. And when I read that, *I* said "Halloa, halloa!" too, I give you *my* word. And not being able to travel at once, owing to being prostrated with the shock, I came along today, just to have a look at Mr Roland Blooming Bleke, and ask him if he's forgotten that he happens to be engaged to *me*. That's all. I know it's the sort of little thing that might slip any gentleman's mind, but I thought it might be worth mentioning. So now!'

Roland, perspiring in the shadows at the far end of the room, felt that Miss Chilvers was overdoing it. There was no earthly need for all this sort of thing. Just a simple announcement of the engagement would have been quite sufficient. It was too obvious to him that his ally was thoroughly enjoying herself. She had the centre of the stage, and did not intend lightly to relinquish it.

'My good girl,' said Lady Kimbuck, 'talk less and prove more. When did Mr Bleke promise to marry you?'

'Oh, it's all right. I'm not expecting you to believe my word. I've got all the proofs you'll want. Here's his letters.'

Lady Kimbuck's eyes gleamed. She took the package eagerly. She never lost an opportunity of reading compromising letters. She enjoyed them as literature, and there was never any knowing when they might come in useful.

'Roland,' said Lady Eva, quietly, 'haven't you anything to contribute to this conversation?'

Miss Chilvers clutched at her bodice. Cinema palaces were a passion with her, and she was up in the correct business.

'Is he here? In this room?'

Roland slunk from the shadows.

'Mr Bleke,' said Lord Evenwood, sternly, 'who is this woman?'

Roland uttered a kind of strangled cough.

'Are these letters in your handwriting?' asked Lady Kimbuck, almost cordially. She had seldom read better compromising letters in her life, and she was agreeably surprised that one whom she had always imagined a colourless stick should have been capable of them.

Roland nodded.

'Well, it's lucky you're rich,' said Lady Kimbuck, philosophically. 'What are you asking for these?' she inquired of Miss Chilvers.

'Exactly,' said Lord Evenwood, relieved. 'Precisely. Your

sterling common sense is admirable, Sophia. You place the whole matter at once on a business-like footing.'

'Do you imagine for a moment—' began Miss Chilvers, slowly.

'Yes,' said Lady Kimbuck. 'How much?'

Miss Chilvers sobbed.

'If I have lost him for ever—'

Lady Eva rose.

'But you haven't,' she said, pleasantly. 'I wouldn't dream of standing in your way.' She drew a ring from her finger, placed it on the table, and walked to the door.

'I am not engaged to Mr Bleke,' she said, as she reached it.

Roland never quite knew how he had got away from the Towers. He had confused memories in which the principals of the drawing-room scene figured in various ways, all unpleasant. It was a portion of his life on which he did not care to dwell.

Safely back in his flat, however, he gradually recovered his normal spirits. Indeed, now that the tumult and the shouting had, so to speak, died, and he was free to take a broad view of his position, he felt distinctly happier than usual. That Lady Kimbuck had passed for ever from his life was enough in itself to make for gaiety.

He was humming blithely one morning as he opened his letters; outside the sky was blue and the sun shining. It was good to be alive.

He read the first letter. The sky was still blue, the sun still shining.

'DEAR SIR,' it ran – 'We have been instructed by our client, Miss Maud Chilvers, of the Goat and Compasses, Aldershot, to institute proceedings against you for breach of promise of marriage. In the event of your being desirous to avoid the expense and publicity of litigation, we are instructed to say that Miss Chilvers would be prepared to accept the sum of ten thousand pounds in settlement of her claim against you. We would further add that in support of her case our client has in her possession a number of letters written by yourself to her, all of which bear strong *prima facie* evidence of the alleged promise to marry; and she will be able, in addition, to call as witnesses in support of her case the Earl of Evenwood, Lady Kimbuck, and Lady Eva Blyton, in whose presence, at a recent date, you acknowledged that you had promised to marry our client.

'Trusting that we may hear from you in the course of post, we are, dear sir, yours faithfully, HARRISON, HARRISON, HARRISON, AND HARRISON.'

THE END

*This edition of P. G. Wodehouse has been prepared from the first British printing of each title.*

*The Everyman Wodehouse is printed on acid-free paper and set in Caslon, a typeface designed and engraved by William Caslon of William Caslon & Son, Letter-Founders in London around 1740.*